A WEEK AT
SURFSIDE BEACH

A
WEEK
AT
SURFSIDE
BEACH

A COLLECTION OF
SHORT STORIES

Pierce Koslosky Jr.

PUBLISHING

Charleston, SC

A Week at Surfside Beach
Copyright © 2019 by Pierce Koslosky Jr.
All rights reserved

First Edition

Printed in the United States

Cover Photo by Lee Rivers at Right Move Photography

ISBN-13: 978-1-952019-00-5
ISBN-10: 1-952019-00-1

I would like to thank every sentient being who has ever crossed my path in this life, and who, in so doing, has made me a better person.

I would also like to thank Stretch—you know who you are—whose coddling of these stories when their shells were thin and forming made all the difference in how they turned out.

Thank you, Candy, my dear one, "who still abides with me."

To Charlie, Sarah, Petra, and Chase—my home team.

And to Kathy Koslosky, who first told me about this magical place.

(I wanted to thank God for all that He has done for me, but I don't have the space.)

Contents

The Prize

WHAT IS A BEACH? IT IS an excuse. For some, an excuse to show off their tanned, young bodies; for others, an excuse to nap. For still others, it is an excuse to get together again and again. To come to a certain place, one that is always the same and each time different. A place that, over the years, quietly adopts them.

The Moores (Fred and Peg) and the Taylors (Don and Linda) saw each other all the time back in Findlay, Ohio; they lived only three blocks apart. But going to the beach was their tradition, a chance to see each other someplace else. What had begun a long time ago as a wild whim, an adventure, was now something pleasant to look forward to, especially when icicles were decorating the leafless lilacs in Ohio.

Like swallows, they returned to the same house every year: Portofino II–317C in Surfside Beach, South Carolina. True oceanfront, it featured four bedrooms (too many for two couples, but so what) and three bathrooms (just right). It was a pretty blue house perched up on pilings for a seagull's-eye view of the ocean. There were windows everywhere on the large, open first floor; you had to close your eyes if you didn't want to see salt water. And that private walkway to the beach was why they tried to never lose "their" week when it came up for rental.

The two couples had only missed coming out together twice in all this time: once for Fred Moore's surgery, and once, near the very beginning, when Laura Taylor was born. Peg (née Thomas) and Linda (née Czernik) were at the heart of it all. They had been joined at the hip since the age of eight years old, when Linda and her family had moved into town from Youngstown. Fred met Don in high school. Don knocked him over while barreling out of the boy's bathroom, having just released a plague of flies that engulfed them both.

Don was a practical joker. The first time the top of the ketchup bottle came off and covered his older brother in sauce and surprise, he was hooked. There are some of these types who find their Moriartys and spend decades in ever-escalating, chesslike competition. And then there are some of the same general breed of character who find their ideal foil—the innocent Costello to their scheming Abbott. That was Don and Fred. Hard to guess how many times Fred was on the receiving end over their forty years together. Seven times seventy? Yet Fred never returned fire. Once he changed his clothes, or shot down the balloon with his car keys dangling beneath it, or recaptured most of the Japanese beetles, Fred usually marveled at Don's effort and his ingenuity. There was even that happy martyr part of Fred that felt flattered to be the special target.

Only once did it nearly come to blows between them: when Peg was the target of the prank. Never mind that the dry cleaners got out the stain; Fred was furious on her behalf. This made for several frosty weeks between the couples. Finally, they all missed each other enough to chance an outing, where Don offered his own brand of apology on the fourth tee of the local public golf course. Fred came back on his swing in a perfect arc, swinging through the ball like da Vinci's Vitruvian Man, only for the small white sphere to explode into a cloud of glitter. After an easily anticipated gasp, the girls cracked up, and soon, so did the dumbfounded Fred. The good-natured torment could resume, but now there were boundaries.

There they were, in Surfside Beach again. Each year, that very first walk on the beach, while the suitcases were still pouting in the house unpacked, was magical. It would be the first of many, but it was the first. The two couples strolled to the pier a half mile down the beach, kicked their feet in the little pools around the pilings, and walked ever so slowly home. It was going to be a good week.

Beachcombing is a great use of vacation time, an allocation that always progresses from too much to too little. This form of so-called relaxation can be exercised in varying levels of intensity. It's a little like birding in its search for the unique, the unspotted—only a stronger back is required. Beachcombers are, by definition, migratory. They can be solitary, in a pair, or even in a flock. They are like the sandpipers that move up and down the beach, always probing, always turning things over. Imagine the penetrating vision of an eagle, only employed at closer range. The practitioners of this enterprise are features of the changing tides. At high tide, it's "first come, first served" for punctual beachcombers. At low tide the ocean plays "now you see it, now you don't," and will soon reclaim anything that isn't discovered.

Discover is the key word. To find a shell or something never seen before. *Discover.* It is a noble word, whose subtext is: *I found it and you didn't.* Your companion makes a breathtaking find in the sand right in front of you, but it is *their* revelation, not yours. There is the discoverer, and then there is merely the witness. Even if the first instinct is jealousy, the person who but witnesses generally feels compelled by a mix of sportsmanship and tribal custom to act thrilled.

Despite this Darwinian component, beachcombing is a pleasant way to see the evening in. Or to greet the morning, walking at early light and filling an empty coffee cup with the day's first treasures. It is an opportunity to slow down and see, and also to catch up and listen. To hear the ocean in a seashell.

The Moores and the Taylors were avid buffs. Every year they brought their discoveries to the small table that doubled as an umbrella stand at the end of their walkway. Peg and Linda used this as their palette. Finds of the day were arrayed in a precise manner, radiating about the umbrella hole. Items were placed by hue. By genus. By uniqueness. Gold and white and pinkish digger shells framed the table this particular week. Razor shells formed internal braces at each corner, with a limpet shell at the angle where they met. A miniature dried-out starfish radiated from the center top. A tiny, desiccated crab scuttled along the bottom. Just a week was all you got to complete your masterpiece. A couple of photos on Friday before the sunset, and a few more Saturday morning before you vacated the place ahead of the maids. The next people will marvel at your creation for a moment and then sweep it all away, setting down their wine glasses. It's their turn; that's the law of the rental beach house.

Right off the bat on Sunday, their first full day, Peg found the little starfish. Don found a lovely whelk, and Linda found almost all of a small nautilus. As the week continued, it seemed that everybody was finding something of note, something worth repeating the discovery of at dinner—everyone except Fred.

Fred was a specialist, working just at the ocean's edge. He was looking for sharks' teeth. They were there, all right. Prehistoric, to make them even sexier. Sixty-five million years old, various species, always black and almost always tiny. The bigger ones occupy a place of prominence in the shell shops. To a non-native, it sounds terribly exotic and exciting, and the Moores and Taylors were non-natives. These shark teeth are not that easy to spot, and the first one you find, you remember. After that, you'll dart your hand into the low, retreating surf a thousand times looking for another. Usually you'll come up with a nice contoured fragment of a shell that mimics exactly the right shape.

They found a few teeth that trip. That certainly doesn't always happen. These finds were deposited in a place of honor, dropped into a wine glass on the kitchen counter. Don found a couple of good-sized ones, and one almost the length of his thumbnail, which was rather large. Fred was indulging a lifelong dream and hoping for an elephant, yet that week he couldn't even seem to catch a rabbit. He tried to be a good sport about it, but it was bugging him. As the week ticked away, Fred began poking in the surf a tad too aggressively. He was always the first of the group to say, "Hey, how about checking out the beach?"

By Wednesday, this gave Don an idea. He shared the mechanics of his scheme with Linda and Peg, hoping to recruit them, but Peg threatened to tell the whole thing to Fred and kill Don's little "joke" outright. Don hurriedly attempted to spackle over their objections. "Fred never has to know" was his gambit. Linda saw right through him and branded the prank "mean." She'd been through this dozens of times with Don. Once he had conceived of the mousetrap, he had to see it spring. Despite his carefully couched protestations, if Don had an opportunity to pull the lever on a trapdoor somewhere, he would always see to it that that lever was pulled.

Thursday, after running a mysterious errand, Don caught Peg and Linda in the kitchen while Fred was upstairs taking a shower. Fishing his hand into a white paper bag, he pulled out a flat white box with Shell World printed on its top and a sticker that read "$79.95." He pried off the lid, and there was a monstrous shark tooth! Don placed it in his hand and it was more than half the size of his palm. The thing was black as ebony. The crown of it was shiny, as though it were obsidian, while the root was a textured charcoal. The tooth was so large that you could see the edges were clearly serrated, like a grapefruit knife. Peg and Linda wouldn't touch it, but they were amazed nonetheless.

Friday came and started to go. The sun began its prearranged descent, which happened that day to also coincide with the ocean's retreat. Out went the tide, and up went Fred's hopes for what he knew must be his last chance at finding something on that particular trip. He rallied the troops, and the foot patrol began again. The slanting sunlight illuminated every sparkle, every shape.

The little posse headed down to the water's edge, intent yet chattering. Being Friday, most people had come off the beach already to clean up, and then head out and take in one last fried-seafood extravaganza. Once they completed their one last run, the Moores and Taylors would do the same. There were a couple of large shell beds the ocean had left behind that afternoon. These mounds of possibility slowed them down considerably. They paused and picked through the piles of broken clams, seaweed, and driftwood as though they were at a flea market.

Don took this opportunity to move ahead and plant the bait, using his toes to tuck the large tooth into the sand for what he hoped would be a very quick nap. He rejoined the group, his absence unnoticed. As they approached the "spot," Don grabbed the elbows of his female companions and pulled them back.

Fred advanced, unattended. He was looking down at the sand and continued talking, unaware that the others were several feet behind him. He almost walked over the tooth, thinking it too big to be anything but a busted hunk of clam. This gave Don a wince. But Fred paused and bent lower, hovering over the target before even attempting to touch it. His forefinger traced around the edge of the thing, and then his fingers pried underneath it. He grasped it and pulled it free just as a little rill of ocean ran up the beach and filled in the void the thing had left behind.

Fred brought the object up to his eyes in the fading light. His free hand brushed away some of the sand clinging to it. It was unmistakable. It was a shark's tooth the size of a shot glass!

It took another moment for this all to register. Then Fred drew in a breath and let out a middle-aged male squeal. "Look! Look! Look!" he shouted, his only word at hand.

The women came forward. Don held back, surreptitiously covering his mouth with his hand. *Don't blow this just yet*, he thought to himself.

Fred was jumping up and down, exhibiting a rhythm and energy he never displayed on the dance floor. He was overwhelmed with excitement.

All three of the others were busy looking at one another. Peg and Linda had a "Now what?" look on their faces.

Don nonchalantly sauntered up to Fred. "Whatcha got there, buddy?" he asked, tapping the shoulder of the other man's dream.

Fred's mouth was hanging open. Speechless, he thrust the large black tooth, with its jagged edges, toward Don. Fred's eyes were wide. He held the object as though it were a piece of the True Cross. Don hesitated. The women looked at him apprehensively. The straight pin he had prepared for this balloon was held firmly between his thumb and forefinger. This was it: the bursting of the bubble that he had practiced in his mind countless times. Now. Stick the pin in.

But there was Fred, his silly, childlike face reflecting the company of angels.

Don clamped his hand on Fred's shoulder. Peg and Linda took in a nervous breath.

"Unbelievable!" said Don to his friend. And then looking at his wife and Peg, he said, "Looks like Fred's buying the drinks tonight!"

The two women exhaled.

All the way back to the beach house, Linda held Don's hand, squeezing it from time to time.

Later, the tooth safely bulging in his pants pocket, Fred was merciless in his interrogation of the other three. "Come on, one of you put it there! I know somebody did," he said to each one of them separately.

"Fred," Don replied, when it was his turn, "a tooth like that would probably cost a hundred bucks, and I don't love you that much."

Don and Linda and Peg entered into a secret society that day.

Over the next years, Fred brought the matter up again and again and again. A grilling was always to be expected on each subsequent trip whenever they passed the "spot" for the first time.

There would be more pranks, many more—the car alarm that mysteriously shrieked when Fred approached his own car, the toothpaste-filled Oreos, the air horn under his chair at his sixty-sixth birthday party—but this was something altogether different. The fellowship held.

Sadly, Peg left them a few years later. Not much longer after that, Don, the mastermind and chief suspect, was called away. When he left, he left with that lever still unpulled, his vow intact.

Little did any of them suspect that Fred kept a secret too. He never told anyone about the crumbled white bag that he'd noticed that next day, jammed into the corner of the beach house kitchen trash can. Only an eclipse of a label and the letters S-H-E-L were visible. He plucked the sack from the trash and flattened it until it read: Shell World. Fred slipped two fingers into the bag and brought out a slip of paper—a receipt for $84.74. He stared at it. He started to get mad, but he just couldn't. Instead, Fred smiled and tucked the evidence right back where he found it, recrumpled the white sack, and dropped it back into the open can. He pushed an empty take-out box on top of it and then released his foot, letting the lid slowly close.

Fred told the story of the shark's tooth to his grandkids a thousand times. The moment he returned from that fateful trip, he'd taken the tooth to a jeweler and had it set in silver, made into a pendant. It was quite striking. Fred wore it always, even though the others teased him that it made him look like a Polynesian king or a pirate. No matter.

And when he talked to those grandkids, he would tell them how large a beast this tooth must have belonged to, how it could have easily swallowed any one of them whole. Stretching out his arms to show how large the jaws would have been, he would lunge forward and squeeze an unsuspecting child to underscore his point. Then Fred would slip the leather cord up over his head and let the children pass it among themselves, beaming at their mouths, agape.

The Inflatable Dragon

JOHN'S BODY DIDN'T LIKE HIM ANYMORE. First, the melanoma, then the arrhythmia, and now the psoriatic arthritis. And yes, he forgot some things—nothing important to him, just some things that seemed important to other people. At eighty-one, he expected some parts of the wagon to be wearing out after all those miles. Even so, he was beginning to feel like the little Dutch boy at the dike. First, one leak, and then another—and John was running out of fingers.

Yes, his body was giving up. But he wasn't.

Eighty-one. Okay, so I'm eighty-one, he thought to himself. *So what?* He'd been seventy-two when he and Helen had hiked up to Machu Picchu. After spending forty-five years building a business from scratch up to an eventual 110 employees, he had just stepped off the board of directors the previous year. Now he was an emeritus—whatever that meant. He found himself the recipient of unwanted deference. Was he suddenly *that* old? Doors were being opened for him. People tried to give up their seats on the bus for him. *Not so fast*, he thought. *Not so fast.*

John made the mistake of complaining about his problems to his kids—pardon, *adult children*. But when talking among themselves, these adult children chose to take his sharing as something more, perhaps a cry for help. Suddenly John's future was on the family agenda. Helen would have just listened, patted his hand, and kissed him on his old bald head, all without a word. But she was gone now, and how empty the place seemed without her; maybe John had shared that too.

Now his fate had fallen into the hands of a committee. His children were nice people, and they meant well, but it was at his expense. Then, one Wednesday night, there they all were in his living room, and he listened to them tell him what was best for him. Safest. Most practical. The easiest—for him, of course. All of this logic eventually boiled down to a place: Mountain View. A community for people just like…him. And close by. They could visit—when they got the time.

Well, all right then.

So a week and a half later, instead of checking into Mountain View with his allotted box of keepsakes, John was on a plane to Myrtle Beach, $7,000 in cash wadded up in his pocket (to stay off the Platinum Amex as long as he could), no return ticket, and blessedly, no one to meet him at the gate. His whole family would be at Mountain View later that day, waiting to see him after he had settled in. It had been a group decision, and the group would be there. Except that John had told each of them that one of the others would be taking him there. In place of himself, he'd left a nice, polite note instructing his family not to worry; it read, "Don't call us; we'll call you."

It was June, but it was still a little early in the season. The traffic wasn't too bad coming out of the Myrtle Beach jetport now. Lots of groups of guys, like the die-hard golf crew that had been on the flight with him; middle-aged adolescents dedicated to escaping their wives, families, and obligations. John chuckled just watching them.

He was pleased that he could book an oceanfront house at the last minute at this time of the year. There had been a sudden cancellation just before he'd called. The place was in a little complex of ten houses, called Portofino II, in Surfside Beach. His house was 317C, a corner unit right on the ocean.

Twenty minutes after picking up his small bag at the luggage carousel, he was in a fire-engine-red Mustang convertible, driving down Highway 17, indulging himself in a naughty smile at the thought of his no-show reception party back in Indiana.

It wasn't much after 2:00 p.m. He stopped off at a Denny's and ordered a chocolate sundae and a piece of blueberry pie. Good. Then it was on to the rental office to pick up the keys. The sheets and towels would be waiting just inside his house's door.

The house was very nice, painted in the camouflage of an ocean blue. While only twenty-three hundred square feet, it seemed big and empty, though not nearly as big and empty as his own home. The kitchen, dining room, and living room were all one open space, divided into territories by a breakfast bar on one side and a couch framed by two white columns on the other. Upstairs were all the bedrooms, save for a small one tucked off from the bathroom on the first floor. There were windows everywhere, facing out to the ocean, and up and down the beach. Much too much for just him, but there it was.

It was still light outside when he sauntered to the end of the private walkway. He left his shoes on the bottom step, his socks tucked into them. Then, after rolling up his trousers, he walked out to the beach. Even with the sun shining, the sand was cool, and the ocean was cold on his feet. He stood at the water's edge and watched the sun dip golden orange and red into the calm wading pool of the sea. It was as if it was the first sunset he'd ever seen. The beauty of it made him think of Helen; he would have so loved to share this with her. He lingered there into the dark, until the moon and the cold wind chased him back up the beach and inside.

He took a closer look around the place. It was well kept. From all the sitting areas and beds, he imagined it must be pretty lively come July. There was just the expected amount of beach kitsch sprinkled around the house. Next to the fridge, a sign with seagulls and beach chairs informed: "You never know how many friends you have until you buy a beach house." That got a little laugh out of him.

He took his sack of linens and toted them upstairs and then made a half-hearted attempt at making one of the beds. The place had dishes and toilet paper and salt and silverware, but nothing to eat. Nothing to drink, either, for that matter. And he was getting hungry again—at his age, an enjoyable sensation. He had driven past a lot of seafood restaurants on his way in, but he wasn't in the mood just yet. There was a little Italian place that looked nice, and it was close by. Italian sounded good. He would skip the grocery store until later, maybe even tomorrow. Leftovers—that could be the plan. Besides, the house was so quiet. Better to get out of here and go hear a little noise before he changed his mind about this whole crazy idea.

He drove to Naples of Surfside, parked his convertible, and went in. It was dark inside—dark wood, candles—but it was warm, inviting. It smelled good too. A manager came up to him at the small front desk and took him back to seat him. He was a young guy, and he seemed a little nervous.

They walked past a booth that held a late-middle-aged couple and a young woman. The girl looked to be well into her twenties, and if she was the couple's daughter, she could have single-handedly laid to rest the question of nature versus nurture. Her off-the-shoulder top revealed a massive bouquet tattooed on her left shoulder, while her chopped, purplish-black hair made a nice contrast to her shiny nose ring. In front of the girl was an open bottle of red wine with the cork barely stuck in its top. As for the middle-aged couple, they never could have been picked out of a police lineup.

"She's telling everyone that she's getting a divorce," the manager blurted at John once they were out of earshot of the booth. "She just invited herself over to their table." The young man gave a nervous little "this-wasn't-part-of-the-training" laugh. "I think she might be on some kind of medication."

Then he left John to sit at a booth of his own. The restaurant wasn't much more than half full. Either coincidentally or on purpose, the young man had seated John with a direct view of *that* table.

John could see that the young woman was literally wringing a scarf in her hands. It might have been a headband or a bandana—hard to say. John was too far away to hear any of their conversation, or even its tone, but the girl was doing all the talking; that much was clear. The middle-aged couple wore identical dazed smiles. Every now and then one of them would make an acknowledging nod. Whether this was volunteered or requested, he couldn't tell.

John wasn't sure what to think. To him, this wasn't particularly embarrassing or shocking, or whatever else it was that was causing his fellow diners to avert their eyes. On one level, it was actually kind of funny. These poor polite rabbits, trapped by their very niceness at a table with this woman, her divorce, and her bottle of wine.

A long time ago, before John had decided to go out and get as rich as he could—apparently so that he could leave as much as he could to those adult children of his—back before all that, John had worked as a psychological assistant (read: orderly) in the mental ward of a big hospital. He was going to college and trying to earn enough money to help cover life's little luxuries, like food, for instance. Those were some of the weirdest and fondest days of his life, and they'd taught him a lot.

This girl wasn't obviously dangerous. The bandana kept traveling up to dab her eyes, but there were no giant, jerky movements. No sudden shouting. Only a lot of tears and talking. She was just…sad.

John felt sorry for her.

He looked around the restaurant. Everyone else in the place was doing a pretty good job of looking away. The closer tables occasionally indulged in staring. Was no one going to come forward and help this girl?

No, they weren't.

John looked down at his hands for a minute or so. Then, still looking at them, he pushed himself up from the table and made himself walk across the restaurant. Before he'd really thought it through, he was standing in front of their booth. He faced the couple, who looked at him expectantly.

"Do you mind if I talk to this young lady for a minute?"

Vigorous head nodding. *Please*, their eyes said.

John now turned to the girl. She was about the age of one his own granddaughters; she had the same kind of nose too.

"Young lady." He almost instinctively called her "Miss," but remembering the manager's talk of divorce, thought better of it. "Is there something the matter?"

Her big red eyes looked up at him. She had been so engrossed with her captives that she hadn't quite taken him in yet. "Bobby. Bobby's gone. Bobby doesn't want to be married. Bobby's gone!" It all came out at once, somewhat smeared together by the wine.

"Have you had your dinner yet?" John wondered.

"Dinner?" the girl repeated absentmindedly, trailing off.

"Would you like to join me?" John asked, his voice pleasant and sincere. "I'm here all by myself."

It would be hard to describe the look that swept over the middle-aged couple's faces when they heard John say this. Maybe something out of Raphael.

The girl cast him a glazed but wary eye. Gazing about the room, she took comfort in all the people in the place.

"Yeah, sure," she said slowly.

John held out his hand. She gave him quite a tug as she clutched it and pulled herself out of the booth. And then pausing, she rotated and grabbed the neck of the wine bottle as she went. Down the aisle of the restaurant they proceeded. She needed a little help from John navigating her way through the narrow passageway, bumping off the occasional banquette to correct her course.

They got to his booth and sat down. It was silent for a few moments as the girl tried to take in the new situation. She was making an effort to get her focus back. John could see that, and it made him glad that he'd invited her.

"Mind if I see what kind of wine you've got there?" he asked politely.

She shook her head and held out the bottle without a word. She was looking at John suspiciously.

He took the bottle carefully from her hands and pretended to inspect it. It was still almost half full. The label was a combination of garish colors and type set in different styles and fonts. It almost hurt to look at it.

"Hmmm," John said, rotating the bottle as tenderly as he would have a sleeping Bordeaux. "Hmmm."

A waiter timidly approached their booth. "Can I get you anything?" he ventured.

John reached across the table for a menu, but before he'd even opened it, the girl blurted out, "Do you guys have calamari?"

"Calamari?" The waiter seemed startled by her sudden demand.

"Yeah, calamari."

"Yes, we do," the waiter said. "Would you like to put in an order?" he asked gallantly.

She looked at John.

"Yes, please," John said cheerily. And off the boy went.

"Thanks," the young woman said, directing it at John.

She seems nice, John thought. When he'd made eye contact with her, he said, "Now what is this about Bobby?"

She looked at him, slightly puzzled. "Do *you* know Bobby?"

"No. No, I don't," John replied. "I don't even know you." He held out his veined hand. "My name is John. What's yours?"

She cautiously took the offered hand. "John," she repeated. "Renee," she said back. "Renee."

"Well, Renee, why is a nice girl like you so upset?"

This stopped her cold. "What do you know?" Her voice now had a sharp note to it. "I'm not so nice."

John shifted uncomfortably in his seat. It was time to change the subject. "Maybe you're not, but you could be drinking a nicer wine," he said, looking over his glasses at the atrocious bottle on the table. He leafed through the menu, stopping at the modest wine list in the back, which was predictably heavy on Italian, with a dash of Californian.

"Hmmm." He ran his finger down the list. "Sangiovese. Barolo. They do have a nice Chianti riserva, but that might be a little on the tart side. They also have a barbera, which will be a little heavier, but it will have nice, forward fruit. Mind if I buy us a bottle?"

Renee took a long look at him. "You trying to get me drunk?"

Her question put John on the verge of blushing. "N-no."

"You're not some kind of perv, are you?"

"No." Now he did blush. "I-I just thought you could use someone to talk to."

Renee slumped back into the booth. "Sorry. Sorry," she said. "Long night." She sighed.

The calamari came, and John ordered the barbera.

"Two glasses?" the waiter asked.

John glanced over at Renee. Renee nodded yes.

"So want to tell me what happened?" John tried again, after the waiter had left.

Renee sighed again and pulled herself back up to the table.

"We had another fight." She shook her head. "I was trying to remember what started it." She paused. "This time it got real bad. Bobby said he doesn't want to be married anymore. And then he just…left."

That hung in the air for a while. Then, noticing John's wedding ring, Renee said in a hopeful voice, "You're married."

John let out a deep breath. "Well, I was. My wife—Helen—she passed just over a year ago."

"I'm sorry."

"That's okay. We had a long, long time together."

"Any advice?" Renee looked at him expectantly.

John felt the responsibility of the moment. *What can I look back and tell her?*

"Renee," he started. "There are no marriage experts, only married people. And every one of those married people will give you different advice. There are no magic answers for anybody."

This seemed to deflate her. "Maybe we got married too young," Renee offered.

"We were much younger than you when we got married. And we did our share of fighting too." John sighed. "We wasted a lot of time that way."

"Not all fights are a waste of time."

"You'd be surprised."

"So what? I'm just supposed to say nothing?" She was getting angry again. And then she got quieter and said, "If we were supposed to be together, we wouldn't fight." Out came a long sigh. "Maybe I should just bail on the whole thing." She dabbed her eyes again with the bandana.

The wine came. At John's suggestion, they ordered an entree to share. Then he insisted that Renee close her eyes and smell the wine.

"Mmmm," she said. He had her keep her eyes closed as she tasted it. "Hey, that's really good!" Renee exclaimed.

He was glad to distract her. *She has such a long time ahead of her*, he thought to himself. *She really is a sweet kid.*

"Listen," John began. "When Helen and I were dating, she smoked. I didn't care. Her kissing was so great, I thought about learning to smoke myself." He laughed. "But she knew that I hated it. I had a favorite aunt who died of lung cancer. It really bothered me. As Helen and I got more and more serious, I hardly ever saw her smoke. I knew she was still smoking, but I let her pretend that she wasn't. Anyway, we got married and still she smoked—more, after two or three years. We had three kids. I used to try and get her to quit. If she saw something that she really wanted, I would tell her I'd buy it for her if she quit. She would promise. I would buy it. And then, after about a week or two, she would start again. And I'd find out and I'd get mad. We were crazy about each other, but this was like a bad game that we kept playing.

"And then one day—this was after I had gotten her a fur coat—she was gone somewhere with the kids and I came across a half a pack of Pall Malls tucked in the back of a drawer in the kitchen. I can still see that pack of cigarettes in my hand. I was furious. I took those cigarettes and cut them up, right out in the open, on the living room table. A real mess. She came home with the kids and walked right into it. It was terrible. She turned white with embarrassment. But just as I was about to yell at her—in front of the kids, mind you—she went from white to beet-red." He clucked his tongue and shook his head. "You could have cooked an egg on her forehead, she was so mad.

"She grabbed the kids—still in their coats—and marched them right back out again. I didn't know doors could slam that loud. After that I didn't hear from her for almost a week. Later I found out that she went to her sister's in Pittsburgh. Days went by, and not a word. I was going nuts. And then one day I came home from work, and I could hear the kids playing in the family room. There she was in the kitchen, cooking. The place smelled like paradise.

"We never said a word about it the whole night. And afterwards"—John's face began to flush—"afterwards, when we had the kids all tucked in, we made up. And I mean we *really* made up." He laughed and Renee laughed too.

"Did she quit smoking?" she asked.

John had a little chuckle to himself. "No." He paused. "But I quit caring about it."

He picked up his wine glass and swirled it into a little red whirlpool. He pushed his handsome nose into the globe and took a deep breath. Then he tilted the glass back just enough to deliver a long sip.

"And then," he said, "about a year or two after that, she just quit on her own." He smiled. "I haven't thought about that pack of Pall Malls in fifty years."

The food came. Veal scallopine, and pretty good too. John asked to have a second plate brought, and then he carefully divided the food. He leaned across the table to deliver Renee her portion.

"So what are you doing up so late, anyway?" Renee asked, her mouth full of pasta.

He laughed at the way she had put the question. "I'm running away from home," he said, somewhat sheepishly.

She gave him a funny look, and seemed unsure whether she'd heard him correctly.

John dropped his voice and confided, "Actually, you're the first person I've told this to."

Then he told her about his kids, about "the decision"—the whole long saga.

"I'm going to be eighty-two years old in two months." He looked at her earnestly. "Do you think I'm crazy, Renee?"

"Nuh-uh," she replied. "It's your life. Why let them tell you what to do? If you can't do what you want when you're eighty-two, when can you?"

"Honestly, Renee, I'm afraid. I'm afraid of what comes next. Afraid of getting old and stuck up on the shelf and forgotten." He paused. "I thought I'd have it all figured out by now."

"Seriously!" Renee blurted out. "Man, if you don't know at your age, I guess I'm screwed for sure!" They both broke out laughing.

They talked and talked until they were the last ones in the place. She had a lot of questions about those well-meaning kids of his. This kind of overinvolved family was new to her. He had questions too. How did she and Bobby meet? How long had they been married? Renee wanted to know more about him and Helen. Back and forth between each other's lives they went. The middle-aged couple had long since escaped. An expressionless older woman began vacuuming all around them. Soon they were lifting their feet for her.

"Are you going to be okay?" Renee asked quietly.

"I will, if you will," John replied.

"Okay, okay," said Renee, smiling. "Hey, thanks for tonight." She picked her purse off the seat and got up to leave. As she passed by him, she placed a hand on his shoulder and bent down and kissed the top of his old, bald head. He blushed. Reaching up, he covered her hand with his own. They held that pose for what seemed like a long while, neither of them willing to move.

He thought for a moment and turned to look up at her. "You got a ride?"

"Mmmm, no, actually."

"Got a place to go?"

She thought a minute. "Yeah. Home. Home sounds good."

He got up from the table and offered her his arm. "May I?"

She gave him a big smile and nodded.

The night was dark, so dark the stars had little trouble poking through the lights of the parking lot. John and Renee were quiet as they strolled out into the late evening. His red convertible was one of the last cars that remained in the lot.

When Renee realized that that was the car they were headed toward, she said, "Eighty-two years old, huh?" She gave him a playful nudge.

John was just about to open the passenger door for her when a pickup truck rumbled right by them, cruising slowly along the side road that ran past the restaurant. The truck stopped. Then it backed up and turned into the parking lot, heading toward John and Renee, the headlights in their eyes. A window came down on the driver's side and a head thrust out.

"Renee! Renee! Baby!"

As the truck lurched into park and the driver's door opened, John and Renee exchanged one last look. She squeezed his hand. "Thanks. Just thanks," she said to him.

Then she ran through the two shining beams of light and into Bobby's arms.

The Pier

T<small>O</small> <small>APPRECIATE</small>—<small>TRULY APPRECIATE</small>—<small>THE OCEAN WHEN YOU</small> see it for the very first time, you have to come from someplace like Nebraska. There they have oceans of corn and oceans of wheat, so the concept of the ocean is already fairly established. But in Nebraska the only big body of water is a lake, and the only actual moving water is a river. To see these forces combined and magnified a thousandfold, and to come from the land of blowing, waving, rippling grain, is to truly appreciate. The Collins were from Nebraska.

The pretty blue oceanfront house they'd rented was not that far from Surfside Pier. That pier was a magnet to Jim. Here was the railroad trestle bridge he had loved since he was a boy, but here, too, was the ocean, running back and forth beneath it. Something fastened to the sea! And something that ventured out into it, looked out across it. Jim was transfixed.

His wife, Donna, was only too happy to indulge him. She was just as much in awe of the ocean; she couldn't believe that they would have a whole week of this. To be making their breakfast and looking out the windows and see the ocean everywhere—it was like a dream.

It wasn't even half a mile to the pier from their house. By sand or by sidewalk you could be there just as quickly or as slowly as you wanted. The pier consisted of a few small shops, anchored by a bait-tackle-souvenir shop on one side and a restaurant stretching out on the other. Even if the food had been lousy, Jim would have found himself there, just to sit at an outside table, just for a view of that gorgeous wooden pier. And for a buck, you could walk out onto it and linger as long as you liked.

The pier had its own little community, its own hierarchy. Scattered on either side as you made your promenade were all types of fisherpersons. Here a beer, there a Mountain Dew; many people smoking, in a place where no one would tell them not to. They pretty much all knew each other; certainly any-one with an ineradicable tan was a full member. Some fished just around the tide, while others ventured deeper. Shrimp was the common bait with the now-and-then-ers; mullet and menhaden were the choices of the more serious. At the far end of the pier, the structure abutted a much wider wooden square, a space reserved for the high priests of this addiction: the king mackerel fishermen. Here were the big rods and the elaborate rigs. At various times and always during a tourna-ment, a garish, yellow propylene rope was stretched across this square, about fifteen feet from its end. No red velvet rope in Los Angeles was as exclusive as this one.

That rope was down today, so Jim and Donna timidly made their way to the very end of the pier. Jim was awestruck by the complexity of these big rigs. One complete outfit consisted of two separate rods and two separate lines, each acting as a sort of anchor for the other. At the end of the money line swam the bait. It was usually a bluefish big enough that Jim would have been thrilled to have caught it. Said bait swam in lazy, unsuspecting circles, with its leader affixed to the secondary line by a plastic clothespin. It was a trap to give the king time to strike and run and set its own hook.

Jim watched a bluefish trace its circles just at the surface of the water. But wait! What was *that*? A huge shape, some six or seven feet long, and thick—it looked like a submarine—neared the rig. It lazed past it, exposing an unmistakable dorsal fin, turned up its white belly, and with a silent thrust of its tail, disappeared. A shark! Jim was in shock. Donna hadn't been looking that way, but surely the half dozen old-timers staring out at their rigs had. Why weren't they panicked like he was? He had just seen an African lion swim by! And yet no one so much as flinched a muscle. And then Jim heard one old character say to another, "Sharks have never been worse," as the man spit into a cup.

And just as he said that, off to the north side of the pier—the side Donna was facing—here came another one. This shark was a little smaller—but not by much—and it came to the surface like it was auditioning for *Jaws*. Up it surged and snapped its tooth-filled mouth onto an unwary menhaden. With its catch in its teeth, it slowly sank back in, turned, and slapped the water with its broad tail, making a loud splash.

She saw that one. "Jim, there are sharks out here!" Donna said in an alarmed hush.

"I know," Jim answered nervously. But as no one paid the great fish any mind, each one intent on the business of their own lines, so Jim and Donna pretended that everything was fine.

Jim later learned in the diner—where everything was southern and everything good—that this was the "new" pier; Hurricane Hugo had gotten the last one in '89. Out there somewhere in the sea was a big old red Coke machine, plucked right off the end of the old one. Jim was surprised to discover that Hugo was also responsible for the complex where they were staying. Prior to that category 4 monster, there had been a couple of unassuming shacks snoozing on that very piece of beach. Hugo had relocated the pair of them to the middle of Ocean Boulevard. Enterprising developers convinced the owners that this was an act of divine beneficence, and voilà! A year and eight months later, just in time for the season: Portofino II.

That diner got to be Jim and Donna's understood, preordained lunch destination. Jim had to take his walk on the pier and see what was going on that day. He was fascinated with the fishing. He had spent enough time sitting on a bank with a pole to be familiar with the basic mechanics. But never at Standing Bear Lake had someone yelled "Here they come!" and then thrown a net over the railing big enough to encircle a Volkswagen. And never before had he seen men haul up that same net boiling over with fish, spilling them onto the wooden pier. And then, with shouts, everyone within hearing was exhorted to run up and grab some—the charity of the gospels in action. Fascinating.

It was a shame that Jim felt too intimidated by it all to actually rent a rod and join in. *I wouldn't know what the hell I was doing.* He witnessed an impressive number of embarrassing snags, many resulting in snapped lines. Looking over the edge of the pier, you could see the log pilings bristling with fishhooks, monofilament line trailing out from them in the breeze. *Nope. This year I'll watch.*

Jim and Donna came back every day. You can't get she-crab soup in Nebraska, and even if you could, you couldn't have that view. They did a dozen other things in the area: Huntington Beach, where you could pretend that humankind had never discovered South Carolina; Broadway on the Beach, unmistakably indicating that they had. But the couple still found themselves at the Pier Diner every day for lunch.

Bless his wife, Donna—she could tell how badly Jim wanted to try his hand at fishing. She watched him ask the more tolerant anglers dozens of questions.

"They rent the rods and sell the bait right here," she said, telling Jim what they both already knew. It was their next-to-last day. "It's not like you'd have to buy anything but a tub of shrimp."

"I know, I know," he demurred, "but I don't know what I'm doing."

"You know more than you think you know."

The power of the well-placed word!

"Well, maybe," he ventured.

"No, come on. Let's give it a try after lunch."

Her broad smile was all he needed to push him over the line. He was excited. Lunch went by quickly.

Sure enough, immediately after lunch he was at the counter, trading his credit card as security for a rental fishing rod. For another five dollars, he got a tub of shrimp that looked like one giant ice cube. Donna had foreseen this contingency and brought an empty plastic ice cream container to soak the rock-hard block until some shrimp could be peeled from its extremities. She also had a little paring knife she'd snuck in her purse. She was going to see her man catch a fish.

Jim got the paper ticket stapled to his cap that signified and certified his status as a genuine pier fisherman; that was worth five more dollars right there. With Donna linked under his arm, out onto the pier the two of them strode.

On this day, the pier wasn't very crowded at all. He'd waited to make this commitment to fishing until the waters turned rough. The die-hards were there, but not all of the dilettantes. Of course at this point, Jim was undeterred. *Less competition*, he might have thought, if he'd been bolder. *Less of an audience*, was his actual thought. They found themselves an unoccupied perch just past the tide break and settled in.

Spirits were high at first. The sky was obliging, streaked gray and white. The birds were equally obliging; a brown-necked cowbird came and took a shrimp tail from right in front of them. But the fish were not as obliging. The little nibbles he quickly jerked back against were all pinfish, in for an easy supper. Jim knew this from talking to the regulars. Time and again he pulled up his line, just to rebait and continue feeding them. Even as some of the other anglers gave up wrestling with the ocean and headed back on their long, empty-handed walk down the pier, Jim hoped for something, some solid, decent bite, at least, to show that he was still held in favor. Alas, no such sign.

Yet another hour went by with nothing but Donna's cheerfulness to break up the growing gloom. The sea was giving up nothing today.

Donna spotted a knot of people on the beach, all pointing toward the pier—or more accurately, pointing under it. Jim couldn't make out their words above the surf noise, but he could see they were shouting.

"Hey, there's a kid in trouble!" Jim heard the guy in the fishing spot next to him say.

The man was straining forward over the railing, looking down at something. Back from the beach, Jim heard a scream break through the muffle of the ocean. A large woman with a Styrofoam swim board under one arm was rushing into the water, waving her free arm and yelling and pointing.

Jim stood up off of his perch and leaned over the railing in front of him. He couldn't see a thing. Donna crossed over the pier and looked over the opposite railing, but couldn't see anything either. But they both saw a red boogie board—a big Spider-Man figure on it—about twenty feet from the pier and floating quickly away from it.

And then up came a high-pitched "Help! Help!" right from under their feet.

"That kid is trapped under the pier!" someone shouted.

"Help!" came the voice again.

A man next to them was on his cell phone. "It doesn't have an address, darlin'; it's the Surfside Pier. There's a kid in the ocean stuck underneath it, and he's in trouble. Send someone quick!"

They still couldn't see the boy; the planks of the pier were too close together.

Donna got down on one knee and shouted, "Hang on! Help is on the way!"

"Help!"

"Hang on, honey!" Donna yelled back. "What's your name?"

"Help me!"

"Help is coming! What's your name?"

"Tanner!"

"Hang on, Tanner!"

A few of the old-timers left their posts at the end of the pier and now craned their necks out over the railing. People moved up and down this little section of the walk, but there was nothing anyone could do from up there. Jim could see that they were anxious.

"If he hangs onto those pilings too long, those fishhooks will tear him up," someone said.

That woman with the Styrofoam bodyboard was obviously the boy's mother. She was stalled in front of the breakers. She wanted to swim out to him but already struggled in water up to her shoulders, helpless.

"Hang on, Tanner! Hang on!" Donna kept shouting.

"I can't! I can't!"

It was maybe eighteen feet from the deck of the pier to the ocean below. No higher, really, than the high-dive platform at the Holdredge Public Pool back home. Jim didn't want to think about the hooks, didn't want to think about the sharks. He didn't say a word to Donna, just fished his cell phone out of one pocket and his billfold out of the other and handed them to her. He kicked off his shoes, and lifted one leg and then the other over the railing.

He stood there for a moment, his hands behind him, holding onto the wood. Then, pushing himself out as far away from the pilings as he could, he jumped.

He landed feetfirst. Under the water he shot, and when he came back up, the rough sea surprised him, and he got a mouthful of saltwater. The current had pulled him away from the pier. He bobbed up and down, and there was Tanner, maybe thirty feet in front of him.

The boy was a little older than Jim had thought, maybe nine or ten years old. He was terrified, clutching one of the pilings directly under the middle of the pier. The waves kept slapping him into the log and then trying to suck him away again. Jim could see that his left hand was cut. A trickle of red ran down across the boy's wrist. Each wave would wash it away, and then it would run back again, a scarlet stream.

Jim could see that if he tried to swim to the boy, he'd get the same battering, maybe smashing into the boy in the process. No good. Jim paddled as close to the pilings as he dared, and then held steady, treading water there.

When the boy realized that Jim wasn't coming any closer, he yelled again. "Help!"

"Kick out to me, Tanner!" Jim yelled above the surf.

"I can't!" the boy shouted back.

"Sure you can!"

"I can't! Help me!"

"Sure you can! Come on, Tanner! I'll get you!"

"I'm not a good swimmer!"

"That's okay! I am!" Jim yelled.

Tanner was scared, but he pushed himself away from the pole. The current carried him through the pilings and into the open sea. Jim swam right up to him. He grabbed the boy around the waist, his arm circling around him. In Jim's firm grip, the boy's fear, now that he was out from under the pier and not alone, seemed to be diminishing. Jim turned them both on their backs, and Tanner kicked along with him as best he could, as they pointed themselves toward the shore. The waves lifted them up so they could clearly see the beach at each crest. Two emergency vehicles pulled up at the top of the dunes, one with flashing red lights, the other with flashing blue ones. Men began getting out of them both.

The ocean shoved them along toward shore. One last big wave swept them through the breakers, and they were in water just above Jim's waist. The big frantic woman was moving sideways through the water to try and reach them. Now their feet were both firmly on the ocean floor, and they were walking their way in. The mom reached them, and Jim let go, letting her have the boy completely.

Men in two different uniforms stood in front of them on the beach, waiting for the boy and his mom to come out of the water. One man had a blanket over his arm; another had already spread a second blanket out on the sand, and some sort of first aid kit was sitting on it.

Jim stopped for a moment in water that was now just around his ankles and caught his breath. There was Donna, running toward him. Looking back out at the sea, he saw a red Spider-Man boogie board heading down toward Garden City.

The Right to Bare Arms

SOMEWHERE ALONG THE WAY, ON THAT long ride from Shenandoah, Pennsylvania, to Surfside Beach, South Carolina, two childhood enemies—now barely teenagers—finally came to a truce. Well, quite a bit more than a truce. Tad Corbett and Jennifer Williams were pressed together side by side, hour after hour, in the back seat of a late-model Chrysler Town & Country minivan. Rolling late at night through nameless parts of Virginia, Tad put his arm all the way around Jennifer's neck, and he kissed her. In the near black, Jennifer watched as the occasional burst of highway lights sparked in Tad's eyes, and that was it.

They were part of a convoy. Two neighbors—friends from a small town in the rolling hills of the Keystone State—had decided to try vacationing together. Take a week at a beach somewhere. The two families ended up accumulating enough other relatives that each tribe needed a castle of its own, so they found a little complex just nine miles south of Myrtle Beach where they could both rent houses. Perfect.

They got their keys just before the rental office closed and headed off to Portofino II (apparently, the Italian Riviera is big in South Carolina). It was a small ten-house affair with a pool nestled right in the center. But they discovered that while one of the houses they'd rented sat smack on the ocean, the other house was across the pool from it, its backside with a breathtaking view of the street. A short tour of the complex by foot, and they realized that the *numbers* on the units—317C was one of the houses they had rented; 315A was the other— were not as indicative of position as the unit *letters*, and C was definitely the letter that you wanted. "Ocean view" for letter A meant if you leaned south off the balcony, you needed someone you trusted holding tightly on to your shirttail.

What to do? It was an awkward situation; of course everyone wanted to be right on the beach, but only four of the ten houses actually did that. As the hour was getting late, somehow a decision was made by somebody—whether on the basis of head count or some other criteria; it wasn't really all that clear—that just for now, just until the office opened in the morning, the Corbetts would take the house on the beach, and the Williamses, the one that could sort of see the beach. Just for that night.

But there was no sorting this all out the next morning at the rental office. All ten houses, oceanfront or otherwise, were booked and already occupied. It was like it or lump it. And with the Corbetts already unpacked, this left the Williamses, who had only nominally unpacked in hopes of a morning move, squarely in the lump it position. Nothing was actually said. No grand gesture was offered; it was all just sort of understood. This pure luck of the draw unfortunately resulted in a suppressed gloat on the part of the Corbetts, and among the Williams, a diffuse, mild bitterness.

This was not a happy petri dish for cultivating the joy blossoming between Jennifer and Tad, but being teenagers, they didn't need any help. They were oblivious. Yet others in their orbit—the smug winners and the sore losers—were not so transported. Discord was strewn between the two houses, and each house knew it. Tad Corbett was forced to hear what bad sports those Williamses were, and Jennifer Williams heard again and again about how grasping and inconsiderate those Corbett people were.

And it was only Monday.

It is a common fallacy that a week at the beach slows you down and forces you to relax, but no family that has actually gone to the beach and rented a house will tell you that this is true. Twelve people in a house renting for $4,800 a week do not relax. They don't have the space to relax, they don't have the time to relax; the sound of the taxi meter running is ever present. All those pictures of people lying idly on the sand are for the tourists. They are pictures of the owners and their families taken in the off-season. In reality, a multiple-family six-and-a-half-day stay in a house half the size of the one they left in Pennsylvania is more like staying in a submarine with a swimming pool attached. That sand on the beach is also the sand running out through the hourglass.

So it took no time in this hothouse environment for bad blood to bloom.

The first blossom took the form of a shoving match: nine-year-old Ryan Corbett versus ten-year-old Ethan Williams. This was poolside on that Monday. No witnesses. No security tapes. However, when Ethan Williams came howling up the backstairs, his face buried in a bloody beach towel, it was clear that he was shy his two front teeth.

In almost every really first-rate conflict, there needs to be some minor, incendiary incident. Moments after Ethan made his sobbing entrance, Mr. Williams had bolted out the door, slamming it shut on Ethan's wail.

"Did you see what Ryan did to Ethan?" he sputtered at eleven-year-old Emily—a Corbett cousin—who just happened to be the one to open the door at 317C.

Debbie Corbett came around the corner from the kitchen. It was clear from the look on her face that her son Ryan hadn't regarded the fight as being newsworthy.

"What's the matter?" she asked innocently.

"Your kid knocked out Ethan's teeth!"

"Ryan!" she called out. And again, "Ryan!" went up the stairs. But Ryan, who had been sitting on the walkway to the beach dissecting a dead crab that he'd found that morning, had disappeared at the sound of Mr. Williams's voice.

"Are you sure?" Debbie offered meekly.

"I'm sure I'm not going to be the one who pays to fix them!" Mr. Williams said with self-satisfied anger.

It must have been this intimation of money that woke Mr. Corbett up from a nap and brought him downstairs. "What's this?" he said to both his wife and Mr. Williams.

The latter answered in a tone just shy of a yell. "Your little thug knocked out my kid's two front teeth, and you're going to pay to fix them!"

Mr. Corbett could not so quickly achieve the beautiful tomato hue of Mr. Williams' face, but he could spontaneously shout, "I'm not paying for a thing!"

Mr. Williams did not hesitate. "You may not *want* to pay," he said darkly, "but you're *gonna* pay." And then he wheeled around and stomped back down the wooden stairs. Moments later, Ethan's lament again briefly escaped as he opened and slammed the door to 315A. The Corbett women phoned the Williams women two or three times trying to sort things out, but the big Keystone Karaoke Knite was dead. The all-family dinner at "The Pirate's Parrot"? Dead. This was war.

In whatever other world that Jennifer and Tad now inhabited, this uproar was viewed with a mixture of why-can't-we-all-love-each-other compassion and an expanding sense of high drama. Not that the course of their love necessarily would have run smoothly anyhow. But from their little pink cloud, they couldn't understand what all the fuss was about.

Unfortunately for them both, their interest in each other was soon detected, just after the Williams-Corbett bout. In fact, Mr. Williams was still warmed up from his visit to Mr. Corbett when he came upon Jennifer and Tad on the other side of the sand dunes. He was standing on the walkway that led from the communal pool, out walking it off after Ethan had calmed down. From the top of the stairs he could see Jennifer's body, but Tad's head was superimposed upon it, connected at the lips. Their arms and legs were amateurishly and inefficiently aligned.

Once he had digested all of this, Mr. Williams unleashed a crimson roar. "What the hell is this?"

Tad jumped up, the goofy, far-off look on his face converting to terror as his fight-or-flight mechanism kicked in, leaving Mr. Williams in a loud Doppler effect behind him.

About two hours later, anyone around the pool could have heard Mr. Williams yell "Keep the hell away from my daughter!" when he caught Tad in the azalea bushes directly underneath Jennifer's room. Her window came down like a guillotine at the sound of her father's voice, and the fleeing Tad got language hurled at him that could have been grounds for a restraining order.

And the following afternoon, when Mr. Williams went upstairs to take his patriarchal nap, he caught Jennifer leaning halfway out of her open window. He came up quietly behind her, and lined up his head with hers. There was Tad across the way, leaning out of his own window, professing his undying love in full-on, silent-screen mode. Tad blew a kiss that traveled across love's chasm, but it was received very differently by the two people in its line of fire. Mr. Williams' sudden presence nearly startled Jennifer right out the window; he had to grab the belt of her jeans to keep her on the second floor.

Mr. Corbett was no fan of this romance either. Suddenly the Williamses were no longer quite good enough. Tad got a lecture about the "wrong kind of girl" that sailed right over his head. Mr. Corbett caught Jennifer straying past what was now acknowledged as neutral territory, and, loudly clearing his throat, chased her back across the demilitarized zone.

On Wednesday, while the Williamses were all eating lunch, there was a loud crash upstairs. Mr. Williams sprang up from the table and again found the window in Jennifer's room wide open. The rock with the piece of paper rubber-banded on to it had chosen to enter the room through the top half of the window, and both windows had been broken. Mr. Williams picked the rock up, and with all the accuracy of a father's ire, hurled it across the courtyard at Tad's dumbfounded face. Tad ducked, but he needn't have; the missile entered the first floor of the Corbett's house by way of the closed dining-room window, and then skipped twice across the table and landed in a glass bowl of potato salad.

The two broken windows glowered at each other all night long, more broken teeth in the war between the House of Corbett and the House of Williams. The workmen sent by the realty office showed up the next day and were promptly pinned down by the verbal crossfire between Mr. Williams and Mr. Corbett. They measured, they left, and when they returned, the two livid men hadn't budged. The workmen parked right between them again. And so it went. The two fathers took to stalking about their respective keeps. Each was on permanent patrol, keeping a lookout for the corresponding undesirable influence. Eternal vigilance is the price of someone else's virtue.

By this point, Mr. Williams and Mr. Corbett had stopped talking to each other altogether. They were both in a full-blown sulk. The families that had come to vacation together were now studiously vacationing apart. Diane Williams and Debbie Corbett found themselves coordinating all this, checking with each other to keep interfamily contact down to a bare minimum. As the next tense days of détente passed by, Jennifer and Tad were reduced to seeing each other at the changing of the guard, their gleaming braces aching for each other.

Diane and Debbie never bought into any of this. Yes, it was their idea to vacation together. Yes, it was their idea to go to the beach. They had even picked out the complex they were in, Portofino II. So they were aghast at witnessing this implosion between their households. Unlike their inflamed husbands, they were already thinking of what this would all mean once they got back to Pennsylvania.

It was Diane Williams who proposed a What Happens in Surfside, Stays in Surfside / What-Would-Jesus-Do dinner. As the matriarch of the more aggrieved family, her olive branch carried extra clout. Since Debbie had been in on it from its conception, the intrafamily lobbying began in earnest. The Lazy Seagull Café, a place just a couple of miles south of where they were, and right on the beach, seemed the perfect neutral spot, since neither family had been there. Last night of the trip; let's be there at 7:30 p.m. They agreed.

A large painted shark to mark the men's room and a corresponding mermaid to indicate the ladies' room—the place looked perfect. So perfect that it was also packed. The wait to be seated turned into an hour and fifteen minutes. This holdup began to take its toll on the forced good cheer. Finally, they were ushered to a long wooden plank with benches under each side. The table was by the door to the kitchen, but there was also an ocean view. *Somehow*—as any number of Williams family members would later say, rolling their eyes to underline the word—the Corbetts all ended up on the side of the table that looked out at a beautiful, starlit night draped above a glistening sea. The Williamses faced the kitchen.

Tad and Jennifer became awkwardly, although not entirely by accident, seated across from each other, spaced one cousin to either side apart. Mr. Williams started to make an issue of their proximity, but Diane reined him in with a stare. He soon became distracted with separating the two boys, who would forever be connected by two lost front teeth.

Of course, the place being so busy, the service was proportionally slow. At last, a young man wearing one of the restaurant-logo T-shirts that were for sale by the front desk showed up with an armload of menus. This action seemed to constitute some unit of service in his mind, as he promptly disappeared after saying, "Welcome to the Lazy Seagull." He didn't return for fifteen minutes. The delay made the small talk shrink smaller and smaller.

Their server eventually did return, ready to share a little more of his time with them. He navigated the coastline of the long wooden table, and ended with the two couples. "Separate checks?" he asked. Oh, indeed.

"I'll have the shrimp and grits," Mr. Williams said, and he rattled off his choice of hush puppies, salad dressing, and beverage.

"I'll have the shrimp and grits," Mr. Corbett said, fighting off the urge to say the word "too."

"Uh, I'll have to check," the waiter said mysteriously, and then disappeared. He was back quickly this time, and without looking at either man, said, "We're out of the shrimp and grits. I only have one order left."

The table got saloon quiet, like when the piano player jumps behind the piano, right before the shooting starts.

"You can have it," Mr. Williams said, responding to a poke from Diane.

Mr. Corbett took a moment to consider what the significance of this offer might mean, and then said, "No, you can have it."

"No, *you* have it," Mr. Williams said too quickly, with all the emphasis on "you."

"You ordered it first," Mr. Corbett responded.

"Hey, I don't need your charity!" Mr. Williams shot back.

Even the waiter was now paying attention. Their whole table was frozen, looking at the two men. But as Mr. Williams stared at Mr. Corbett, he noticed that the other man was looking past him. Something over his own shoulder had caught Mr. Corbett's attention—something out on the beach below them.

Mr. Williams turned in his chair and dimly saw two people, though they were so entwined that it was hard to tell at first. They were kissing. Whipping back around, Mr. Williams did a quick census of the table. Two empty chairs. He launched from his seat and headed to the back of the restaurant and out the door.

It took Mr. Corbett a couple of moments to catch up with what was going on. He craned his neck toward the beach, and now recognized his son locked at the lips with that Williams girl—and took off after Mr. Williams.

Even though Mr. Williams had him by several furlongs, the first man had left a startled wake through the restaurant as he'd exited, and Mr. Corbett used it to his advantage.

Out in the warm, star-filled night, two young hearts were suspended in the heedless aspic that is love. Forbidden. Delicious.

All at once, Tad felt an enormous yank backward on his left shoulder that completely uncoupled him from Jennifer and sent him tumbling to the sand. Mr. Williams looked too mad to speak. He reached down at Tad, but as he did so, Mr. Corbett's hand clamped down on his own shoulder and spun him around.

Startled and still furious, Mr. Williams stared at Mr. Corbett. In that instant, his unreturned lawnmower, the broken drill returned with only a "Sorry" as compensation, and the memory of every unpicked-up restaurant check flooded over him. Without a word, he sent his middle-aged fist deep into Mr. Corbett's unsuspecting and inviting gut. Mr. Corbett crumpled down on top of the fist, grabbing it with both of his hands. Once his knees hit the sand, he fired off a retaliatory strike. The effect was the same on Mr. Williams, and now the two men were eye to eye. They lunged at each other, grappling in the cool sand of the dunes.

By now the brightly lit windows of the Lazy Seagull were standing-room only and packed with spectators. Tad and Jennifer were nowhere to be seen. Debbie and Diane ran down to the beach, their shoes in their hands. Out of the back of the restaurant came a small cadre of young men in their logo shirts.

Mr. Williams and Mr. Corbett rolled in the sand, swinging wildly at each other with only errant effect. They puffed and punched, but there was little damage. The waiters were soon on them, pulling the two wheezing men apart and pinning their arms behind them.

Even before Debbie and Diane reached their husbands, bright red-and-blue lights whirled out over the top of the dune. Without an attendant siren, the pulsing lights gave the whole scene a disco flavor. Two doors slammed. The women got to their men the same time as the officers did. Mr. Williams's bloody nose and Mr. Corbett's ripped shirt did the talking for them. The cops took over from the waiters, and soon the two old sumos were being led up the beach and tucked into the back of a squad car emblazoned with a palm tree on its side— and off they drove.

It got quiet on the beach. People began drifting back to the restaurant in a slow, murmuring procession. At last, only Debbie and Diane were left, their shoes dangling from their hands by the straps.

Debbie put her arm around her friend's shoulder. "Help you pack?"

Up on the pier, a million light-years away, two distant, willowy figures walked hand in hand, bathed in the tender light of the moon.

Lucy

FIGHTING, FIGHTING, FIGHTING. NEVER A VACATION from the fighting. They'd had this particular one about a dozen times already—the fight about her brother—and here it was again, at the beach. It was probably the reason why their little camp had so much real estate around it. The beach was packed—except for anywhere next to them. By that point in the week, all the beach regulars knew their routine.

Their kids knew it too. Spread out in age from three to eleven, all four of them were off on their own, while Mom and Dad shook the pillars of the earth under a big blue rented umbrella. The two boys were digging down deep into the beach, intent on constructing an ambitious fortress. Sally was decorating a sand shape of some sort with shells and a gull feather. And little Lucy was running in circles with her airplane arms out, trying to catch whatever breeze there might be in the heat.

"It's bad enough I've got to give him money. I don't have to like the guy!" Roger sputtered, pulling at the end of his small blond beard in agitation.

Their fights were always in slow motion. A smart-ass crack. Then a pause. A sharp retort. Then a pause. Maybe then, the wounded act. Even the occasional use of a physical prop. And on and on like that, stretching out whatever the thin plot was that time.

"We have so much," Cindy said. "Why do you always have to be so cheap about everything?"

"Listen, we have so much because I don't waste what we do have," Roger said. "Giving money to your brother is a waste. It's stupid."

"So now I'm stupid, that's it?" she said, glaring at him.

He caught her glare and volleyed it right back at her. "I didn't say *you* were stupid. I said giving that jerk money was stupid."

"He's not a jerk." She bristled. "Why can't you even try and like him?"

"I'd like him a little better if he wasn't so happy to take my money."

"Fine," she said. "Then *I'll* give it to him. I'll give it to him from my own money."

"Great. Now what is that? What is the point of that?" Roger was tugging at his beard again. "You'll just take it out of my pocket with your other hand."

"Asshole!"

"Oh boy. Here we go again." He paused. "You're a little early today, you know that?"

She didn't answer. Well, she answered with a color—red.

One of their boys, John, stuck his head in under the shade of their umbrella. "Mom, where's Lucy?"

Cindy sat up in her chair.

"What do you mean, 'Where's Lucy?'" Roger said. "I thought you were watching her."

"Nuh-uh," John replied. "We're making a fort."

Roger and Cindy froze for a moment. They ducked out from opposite sides of the big umbrella and straightened up. Each of them looked up and down the broad beach, their eyes moving slowly, deliberately, ranging farther and farther out from their own small spot. Blanket by blanket, they sorted through the crowd, trying to make out all the little girls' faces for as far up the shore as they could see. No Lucy.

They started getting panicky, Roger first. They kept looking and looking. Up and down, down and up, again and again. Nothing. They yelled, "Lucy! Lucy!" But they couldn't shout as far as they could see. They turned slowly, facing opposite directions, yelling louder and louder, their voices fading into the noisy, crowded beach.

There was a lifeguard tower a little more than two hundred feet up the beach. Roger ran to it. Cindy could see him pointing and waving his arms. Even at that distance, she could see the lifeguard reach down from his chair and pick something up; it had to be a phone.

Cindy gathered up the rest of the kids and herded them up toward the lifeguard tower. She was trying to distract them, but she wasn't doing a very good job. Sally looked pretty scared. Even the boys were nervous. Nobody knew what was supposed to happen now.

Waiting, waiting. Where were the cops? Cindy and Roger made little eye contact, lost in their own dark thoughts. A crowd had started to form around them, people attracted by their panic.

The police were there in fewer than ten minutes. Two big, fit-looking men in uniform came walking down the beach toward the lifeguard tower. Their polished black shoes looked so out of place in the sand.

"Mr. Collins?" the older of the two officers said, as he turned from the lifeguard to address Roger.

"Yes," Roger replied.

"You reported a three-year-old female child missing—missing from this beach? Is that correct, sir?"

"Yes, officer. What do we do?" Roger asked. He was emotional now; it showed.

"Let's get some information," the officer said in a very calming voice. "Give me a name and description, please." He had a small notebook flipped open, ready to write.

Cindy leaned away from the other children and spoke up. "Her name is Lucy. She has red hair and blue eyes. She's only three," she said, imploringly.

"What was she wearing?" the cop asked.

"Uh, a bathing suit," Cindy started. "I'm trying to remember which one…" Her voice trailed off.

"SpongeBob, Mom," their son James said.

"Yes, that's right," said Cindy, more confidently. "A pink-and-yellow, SpongeBob SquarePants bathing suit."

The other policeman spoke. "Which of you saw the child last?"

"Uh."

"Uh."

Cindy and Roger looked at each other, embarrassed.

"Well," tried the cop, "when was the last time that you remember seeing her?"

They were both red-faced now.

"We came out at ten thirty this morning," Roger offered.

"We would have been having lunch soon," said Cindy, to no real point. "We ate just before we came to the beach."

"Uh-huh," said the cop who'd been doing all the talking. He looked at them both and said, "The best way to handle this is if we have both of you looking for her. I want one of you to stay right here with Officer Tilden and your kids. I want the other one to come with me in the patrol car and ride around the neighborhood, and see if we can't spot your little girl."

"I'm staying!" both Roger and Cindy said at almost the same time. They surprised each other and the officers, but neither of them wanted to leave the place where they had last seen Lucy.

The older officer looked at them closely. He judged Cindy to be the more upset of the two. "Listen, Mr. Collins, why don't you come with me and let your wife and Officer Tilden keep checking the beach for now?" He paused and turned his attention to Cindy. "We'll check in, ma'am," he said to her. "Promise," he added reassuringly.

Before Roger and the policeman could head off, they heard, "Officers! Officers!" An older man was huffing his way up the sand toward them, waving his arms.

When he reached them, he took a big breath, bending forward and holding himself up with his hands braced on his knees. "My wife and I walked up the beach from way down by the Holiday Inn," the man said. "When we got up here, we saw all the commotion and we heard about the little girl." He paused, looking them all over, knowing this was his one line.

"My wife saw a couple leading a little red-haired girl off of the beach."

The cops looked at each other.

"Sir, can your wife show us exactly where they exited the beach?" the older cop asked.

"Yes," he answered. "I can, too. It's that last beach entrance before you get to the Holiday Inn. Know the one?"

"Yes, of course," said the officer.

The old man had been looking down the beach, and now he pointed. "Here's my wife!"

An older woman was moving gingerly toward them. Her husband went back down the dune to help her up the slope.

"Did he tell you I saw them?" were her first words. "I saw them take that little girl," she said, still out of breath.

"Can you describe them, ma'am?" the cop asked.

"I don't know them, if that's what you mean. But I know where they live."

Again, both patrolmen looked at each other.

"You do?" one of them asked.

"Yes. They come out of a little run-down house on the third row. I've seen them toting their stuff past our place all week."

"Can you point the house out to me, ma'am?" the older cop asked.

"Certainly."

He considered his options. "Ma'am would you mind coming with me?"

The woman nodded her assent and straightened out the kerchief on her head.

The officer looked at Cindy. She had been so adamant about staying here at the beach, but of course this sighting had changed everything. She had an anxious look on her face.

The cop took a deep breath. Facing Cindy, he said, "Mrs. Collins, I think you had better come with me." He turned and looked at Roger, and uttered the softest of commands: "Mr. Collins, maybe it's best if you remain here with Officer Tilden. We'll stay in contact."

Roger started to object, more from habit, but the look on Cindy's face kept him silent. "Please do, officer," he said earnestly. Roger and Cindy looked at each other, their eyes pleading.

The cop helped the two women—one on each arm—climb up the dunes to the squad car. He had Cindy sit beside him, while the older lady directed him from the back seat, sitting over on the right.

It was a short mile from where they left the beach to the Holiday Inn. The patrolman drove the two-lane road well under the limit and with no flashing lights. Cindy swept her eyes back and forth in all directions. Just before the street curved inland, they passed the final public access to the beach—two wooden posts in the sand, wide enough to let people through, but close enough together to keep out cars.

As they got near to the circular drive that branched off to the hotel, the older woman said from the back, "No, don't go in. Turn. Here!" and she pointed up the road that fronted the place.

"And now left here." She pointed again.

Cindy was watching the woman closely.

"There!" she said, leaning right up to the mesh separating them and pressing her finger against it. She pointed toward a small, brown ranch with not much of a yard.

The cop pulled the car under a tree in the front yard, where there might have been a driveway but wasn't.

"Would you come with me, Mrs. Collins?" he asked. He looked at the other woman as he said this, the tone of his voice intent on keeping her in the car. She settled back in her seat.

Cindy got out. She walked behind the officer up a weedy gravel path that cut through a parched, brown lawn and ran straight to the front door. There was neither patio nor porch.

The officer knocked on the blistered white door. He did not bang on it, but he knocked for several seconds. There was a pause, and then it was opened by a stooped old man in a short-sleeved, plaid shirt. Before the door had swung open all the way, and before the officer could speak, both he and Cindy could see across the tiny place to a worn, flower-patterned couch. There sat a little, white-haired woman, the matching counterpart of the man at the door, and a little girl with red hair. The two of them were both laughing.

"Lucy!" Cindy shrieked, rushing past the cop. Her voice was so loud and emotional that it startled the child.

The little girl began to cry. She stared at Cindy. "Mommy?"

Cindy ran the few steps over to her and hugged her up off of the couch. Her happy tears flowed into Lucy's frightened ones.

"Where did you go, sweetie?" Cindy asked, stroking Lucy's hair over and over.

"I just walked and walked, and I couldn't find you!" Now she seemed to be remembering, scared again.

"Ma'am," the patrolman said, addressing the old woman, "please tell me how you came to have the child."

The woman had been taking this all in but didn't seem the least flustered. "Why, my husband and I were leaving the beach, and we saw this little girl all by herself. She was crying." She smiled at Cindy and Lucy. "There was no one around who knew the little thing. We took her with us just so she wouldn't be alone. We certainly were going to call you, officer." Now she seemed a little self-conscious. "I, uh, she—" The woman pointed to a small plate full of crumbs that was sitting on a Formica table. "I just gave her a little snack," she said, sheepishly. "I always try to have a cake around."

That seemed to satisfy the officer. He looked at Cindy. She was weaving her fingers through Lucy's red curls, while the little girl rested her head upon her mother's shoulder, all at ease again.

"Any questions, Mrs. Collins?"

Cindy was embarrassed. She imagined the trouble that her neglect might have caused the old couple. The man had moved across the room and was sitting next to his wife now, petting her hand. Looking at the two of them, she thought of herself and Roger.

Roger! He was back there on the beach with the kids. He must be as terrified as she was just minutes ago. How worried he must still be! She thought of how relieved he would be when he was told that Lucy was safe. She could imagine how he would feel when he heard that. Cindy wished that she and Lucy could instantly travel to him and be there to share that with him.

"Any questions, Mrs. Collins?" the cop asked again. "I think we're done here."

His voice brought her back into the room. She asked him, "Have you called your partner yet?"

"No," he answered. "I was just about to."

"Can you please—*please*—let me be the one to tell my husband?" she asked, pleaded.

The emotion in her voice seemed to catch the officer by surprise. Whether or not it would have been out of the ordinary to do so, the look in her eyes settled the matter. He unclipped his phone from his shoulder, pushed a button on it, and handed it to her.

Swimming Lessons

WHAT AM I DOING HERE? BOB thought to himself, as he sat on a plane with three teenage boys, heading from Atlanta to Myrtle Beach. It was a legitimate question. The last few weeks had been completely out of control. Bob couldn't believe that it was Dean, their eighteen-year-old son, who had gotten in trouble. *Trouble?* Actually, *felony* was the legal term. Everyone in their neighborhood was talking about the Gaynors' house getting broken into and robbed. Had Dean not sent that brag pic to his horrified older sister—who had immediately called Bob— no one ever would have known it was him. The cops all told him that; certainly no one would have ever found the money. This was the arm wrestle between Bob and Dean: "Why did you do it?" versus "Why did you make me turn myself in?"

During the ensuing nightmare of police, lawyers, and finally the judge, Bob felt like he was sliding down the face of a sand trap, clawing and clawing at the sand but still sinking down. He hired lawyers, lined up character witnesses, and did everything that he could think of to keep Dean from a jail sentence. So many scared and sleepless nights.

Dean showed a thousand emotions throughout the course of the ordeal, but none of them was remorse—or even gratitude, for that matter. Bob was mad at his son for that and for what the boy had put he and his wife Rachel through. Dean seemed to take this all so lightly, now that the cops and the lawyers and the judge were all behind him. There would be the community service, but that was ahead, and the restitution, but Bob had already paid that.

Worst of all to Bob, it seemed that Dean had learned nothing from any of this. He didn't seem scared at all by the enormity of it, so Bob was scared on his son's behalf. He couldn't stop lecturing him. "You have *no* idea. You have no idea what *could* have happened to you!"

What is it going to take, Bob thought to himself, *to get this kid to take life seriously?*

And then, after all of this mess, after all of the shouting and the tears, this week at the beach popped up. And since his wife already had the ticket to go see their daughter Shannon in London, and since Bob's brother couldn't use the beach house during the week he had already paid for…well, it would be a shame to let this week go to waste. Besides, if anyone needed a vacation right now, it was Bob. So there he was, helping to take up all of row seven on the little plane, along with Dean, his younger brother, Kyle, and Mark, their mutual childhood friend from down the block.

They were pretty close to Myrtle now. It was July, so the plane was packed, and the one bathroom on board was smaller than a steamer trunk. The little jet began bouncing its way down through late afternoon thunderstorms like a Slinky descending a concrete staircase. "Whoa!" the boys kept yelling, attempting to project excitement rather than fear. They soon bumped completely through the black clouds and touched down on a freshly soaked runway. The four of them walked out into the thick, humid summer air and crossed the tarmac to the waiting air-conditioning.

When all their bags were back in their possession, they took their places in the long rental car line. The boys were vocal about renting something "cool"—not some stupid van. Bob was tempted. He was the adult, so theoretically he could do anything he wanted, couldn't he? Theoretically, of course. But as much as he wanted these teenagers to think of him as cool, the mathematical logic of a minivan was oppressively irrefutable. In the end, Bob was going to have to be just as cool as a minivan.

"Man, we might as well be at home," Dean said, as they clambered into the Dodge Caravan, just to rub it in.

The rental house was only about nine miles away once you came out of the cloverleaf and were headed in the right direction—but these were nine Fourth-of-July-weekend miles. The initial three lanes pinched into a two-lane pipeline that took them to the beach, and it was clogged with traffic almost from the moment they left the airport. It took them forty-five minutes of their allotted seven days and six nights just to crawl down to Surfside Beach. But it didn't matter. There were girls in a lot of the cars that were moving alongside their stupid van. That's all that mattered to the two older boys, to the frustration of Kyle, who kept trying to distract them from trying to look cool. Girls the boys' age, girls a little older, even pretty middle-aged moms. Something for everyone.

During occasional brief patches of no one to show off for, the boys resumed their constant shoving. There had to be un-remitting, aggressive contact between them at all times. And with seat belts, height was somewhat compensated for, so the shoving was more egalitarian.

They were all happy, in one way or another. Dean had left his big mess back home, and he didn't have to think about it because he wasn't back home. Kyle was happy just to be in-cluded and to have a couple of extra years conferred upon him temporarily, away from the rigid caste system of public school. Mark, who was between Kyle and Dean in age, was happy to be out from under his own parents' watch. And Bob? The tension between him and Dean was at times palpable, but even Bob was happy, to be honest about it. With Rachel in London, Bob looked like a hero, just for taking all the boys on this ab-surd trip. And this was all so much simpler than the circus he had left behind. Simpler. Simpler.

They made a strange stew, the four of them. Bob was more of a reference point, an axis rather than a chaperone. Sort of an ATM with car keys. Trying to get into the spirit of the thing, he had a couple of outings planned in his head, if not quite actually scheduled. Yet while expectations for the next six days were stratospheric among the boys, staring at the beach and not answering the phone was his big wish.

They turned off the slow-moving parade and headed for the rental agency to pick up the house keys. Then, at last, they were on their way to the little complex that included their own freestanding unit. The boys were vibrating as they rolled down along the road that paralleled the Atlantic Ocean. They pulled underneath the blue house sitting up on stilts. Three boys shot out of the minivan as soon as it came to a complete stop, running up the steps of the walkway to the beach, and leaving Bob to stare at all the suitcases jammed in the van. *What the hell?* he thought to himself, dropping both the bags he'd just picked up. He headed to the beach to be with them.

The sand pouring into their sneakers didn't slow the boys down at all. They went tearing down the beach in the direction of a big pier that waded out to sea about a half mile down from their house. Once Mark had picked up maximum speed, Dean swept down from the dune above him and sent him flying.

"You are dead!" Mark bellowed, as he grabbed two handfuls of sand—impromptu weapons—and took off after him. Bob could see most of this, but they were out of earshot.

"Hey, guys! Guys!" Bob panted when he finally caught up to them. They were already all the way down to the pier, standing underneath the structure, gaping at the large, rolling waves. Their sneakers were soaked.

"Come on," Bob urged, "we have all that stuff in the van to unload. Let's get it in the house and make camp."

Kyle and Mark looked at each other and then at Dean. "Okay," Dean muttered. "Okay." When the older boy started to walk back, they fell in behind him.

Bob followed them off the beach and down to the van. Once saddled with their gear, they all trudged up the wooden stairs, Bob lagging behind to prevent deserters. Then he pushed to the front of the group with a key jutting out from between the bags in his hand, and into the house they poured.

The view stopped them all short. The first floor was bank after bank of windows; everywhere they looked, there was the ocean.

Outside all those windows, they could see that the summer thunderstorms they'd flown through earlier had regrouped and caught up with them. Darkness fell over the house. And here came the rain. Not a Michigan kind of rain, but sheets of rain, buckets of rain, drops of rain the size of peanuts. And thunder. And really wicked lightning everywhere. The broad, flat expanse of the ocean served as a subwoofer. First the crack—like a broom handle breaking next to your ear—then cue the tympani. Each of the boys stood at his own panel of windows, hypnotized. This amazing display went on for several minutes before the kids got bored and Dean turned on the TV. Eventually, the storm got bored, too, and settled back into a slow, steady rain. The boys didn't notice.

Now what? While the All-Seeing Eye had the boys frozen, Bob thought he better get a few things ticked off of his loosely drawn mental checklist. As he already knew would be the case, there was nothing to eat in the house.

"Anybody want to come with me to the grocery store?" No answer. When he started to actually leave, it broke their concentration.

"Get Pop Tarts! Double fudge!"

"Get chips! Tostitos!"

"Rice Krispies!"

The Piggly Wiggly was packed—so packed that the checkout lines backed all the way up into the aisles, gridlocking the shopping cart traffic. Deciding what constitutes "a week's worth" is not the type of mathematics suited for the male mind. There is always the tendency to excess; it is inbred as a mate-attracting characteristic and cannot be turned off. Toilet paper, soda, cereal, chips, milk, and some frozen pizzas to imply that they were capable of using the oven. Shackleton would have been extremely grateful for half of what Bob had in that cart.

"Who's going to help me?" Bob yelled up the stairs when he got back to the house. Nothing. He leaned into the minivan and honked the horn. Still nothing. A thin woman on the porch of the house next to theirs gave him an ugly stare. He had a little more luck with his plaintive cry when he got to the top of the stairs. The skinny plastic handles on the heavy bags were turning the tips of his fingers white. Mark, aware of his undefined status, came sheepishly to the door and let Bob inside.

He could see that the boys hadn't moved a centimeter in the whole time he'd been gone. *We've got to get out of here*, Bob thought to himself.

"Hey, what's for dinner?" Dean asked, without turning his gaze from the set.

That was Bob's cue. He stopped putting stuff away and pulled out a phone book from under the pile accumulated beneath the wall-mounted phone at the end of the breakfast bar. "What are you guys in the mood for?" Silence. Bob thumbed through the yellow restaurant section. Flipping around, he saw a picture of an Asian chef about to catch a bowl in his chef's hat, the object hovering above his head. A teppanyaki place. "Misomoto: Where Dining is an Adventure." He called and got a reservation—much later than he would have liked, but, hey, it was the Fourth of July.

"Have a bowl of Rice Krispies," he advised the room. Then he lifted out a tall, clear bottle of nondescript vodka with a convenient screw-top cap from one of the grocery bags, took a small glass out of the cupboard, threw some ice into it, and went upstairs.

They pulled up to Misomoto about fifteen minutes early. Every bit of that and then some was used up just circling the lot waiting for a parking space to open up. The white pea gravel popped out from under the minivan's tires, the tempo faster, slower, faster, as they orbited. Finally Mark caught sight of a pair of backup lights, and they zoomed to them in reverse in time to lay siege to the spot.

"Boys, go on in and give them our names," Bob said to Mark and Kyle as they all disembarked. "I want to talk to Dean a minute."

Mark and Kyle remained in idle, their eyes on Dean. Dean sighed loudly and slammed the car door. "Oh God. Here we go again." The two boys hustled off to the restaurant. Dean looked at his dad with an expression that was supposed to convey indifference. "Now what?"

It had the desired effect.

"Listen, mister." Bob didn't try to hide his irritation. "This trip is not some kind of reward for all you've put us through. You need to fix that attitude. Don't be so rude."

Dean stared back at him. "You mean rude like this?" His face flushed, but then he wheeled around and took off at a lope to catch Mark and Kyle.

Bob stood by the minivan, letting the heat of the moment flare off. He was not about to lose self-control. There wasn't anything he could think to do about it anyway. He was stuck once again. Letting the air out of himself, he followed after the boys into the restaurant.

The place was packed. It became clear once he'd talked to the hostess for the third time that Misomoto never turned down a "reservation," preferring a roomful of angry customers to the possibility of an empty table. The boys were clumped together and standing by a waterfall that was illuminated by a strobe light. The effect was hypnotic, as droplets vibrated their way down from the top of the stream, paused, and then appeared to start marching back up again. Amazing.

Bob walked over and stood with them a minute, Mark and Kyle separating him from Dean. "It's going to be a while," he said unnecessarily. Then he left them and got a drink at the bar adjacent to the waiting area. There was plenty of time; he got a second.

Eventually they were combined with another group of four people to make the required party-of-eight molecule. It was a couple and their two teenage daughters. The boys took note. They were all led at long last through the beaded curtain and back to their table. The table was a booth that was not unlike a horseshoe-shaped hot tub with a rectangular grill in its center.

Bob ordered a white bottle of hot sake. That was gone before the miso soup was gone, so he ordered another. Well into the little show that the chef was half-heartedly putting on, he got a third bottle. The chef tossed a bowl full of shrimp tails into the air, catching them in his high, starched white toque without any expression on his face. By the time the check arrived, Bob had to have Kyle do the math on the tip and the total, although the numbers Kyle gave him didn't match the numbers he wrote down.

After the bill was taken care of and Bob had picked his credit card up off the floor for the third time, he hoisted himself up from the hot tub and maneuvered his way through the restaurant, the boys following along, watching him and talking among themselves. It was pretty obvious once they were out in the open, free of any supporting walls, that Bob was failing the field sobriety test. *Can I do this?* Bob wondered, as the parking lot swirled around him.

He got to the van and placed one open hand on the side of it to steady himself while he rummaged through his pockets for the keys. Laying hold of them, he lunged for the door lock. He missed his target and lost his balance, dragging the key against the door panel as he slid his way to the ground. A deep silver arc through the paint recorded his trajectory. "Really?" shouted Bob, looking up from his knees at the vivid gouge. He grunted, pushed himself to his feet, and took aim with the key again.

Dean walked right up to him and wrapped his hand around his father's. "Dad. Here, let me help," he said protectively.

Bob turned his gaze toward his son. When Dean smiled at him, Bob smiled back. He released his grip on the keys.

"Yeah. Good idea." Bob laughed. He leaned against the van and navigated his way to the passenger's side, his hand never leaving the sheet metal, pausing only to shoo off Kyle, who had come up to assist him. "I'm good. I'm good," he said, laughing just a little as he climbed up into the seat. Dean drove them home, Bob sometimes humming, providing an echo from time to time to whatever was on the radio.

So much for day one.

He felt like hell the next morning. The sun was sarcastically bright and screaming in through the open blinds. He couldn't remember getting home, let alone getting into—or rather on top of—the bed. It was obvious that the boys had helped him. They'd only taken off his shoes, which were sitting on the floor in front of the bed, laces still tied, but they had draped a comforter on top of him.

Bob made his way down the hall and then down the stairs to the kitchen. The house was completely quiet. Perhaps out of habit or perhaps out of need, he made a whole pot of coffee. The boys must have been up a long time after they'd put him to bed; the sink was piled with dishes. Good—they'd be asleep until who knew when, giving him plenty of time to come back to the planet. Maybe they'd sleep until it was too late to go parasailing; this was not the day Bob wanted to get yanked off the deck of a small boat and shot four hundred feet into the air. No. *What time was it?* Ten o'clock.

The boys slept late enough, all right. And with some coffee, some Tylenol, and some time with his head flopped back in a chair, Bob started to feel a little better. It was Mark who came downstairs first, and that was at almost 1:00 p.m. He didn't seem to be aware of Bob as he scrounged up a pair of Pop-Tarts, took them out of their silver bag, and dropped them into the toaster. He looked directly down into the thing while they cooked, the rectangles of heat seeming to revive him, like a lizard on a sand dune. Then he saw Bob.

"Hi," Mark said, and turned back to look down into the red-orange glow.

It was just about 2:00 p.m. before both of Bob's own sons lumbered down the stairs.

Eventually they did make it out of the house. It was late in the afternoon when, on a sudden group whim, they pulled into the parking lot of Mazemania. A huge square of eight-foot-tall stockade fence contained the maze, which was comprised entirely of the same unpainted fencing. There was a viewers' platform up a flight of stairs with a little snack bar and tables at the top. This overlooked the entire ninety-degree-angled kingdom.

Bob paid for the boys and then headed topside to watch them wander about on the hot concrete below. First Dean and then Kyle figured it out, popping out on the far side of the thing and then joining Bob upstairs. Poor Mark got caught in the same circular logic time and time again, always turning up at the same dead end. Kyle and Dean thought this was hilarious, taunting their friend with the ice cream cones they were eating. Frustrated, Mark had a complete meltdown. He pounded his fists on the rough wood until he got a rather vicious splinter, which instantly metamorphosed his emotional pain into the physical. Bob had to shout down turn-by-turn directions from above to get him out.

That night they ate at the Surf Shack, where everything but the drinks was fried. It was a friendly enough evening, with Bob and Dean in a state of undeclared truce. Bob had at first hoped that in this neutral setting—this gorgeous setting—that Dean would open up to him, apologize, repent—*something*. Dean was instead making it clear that he had no intention of even thinking about the upheaval he'd single-handedly created back home. Rachel was so upset that she was still talking about moving out of the neighborhood. This taken-for-granted surreal trip was getting on Bob's nerves. He had a couple of beers, but they had little impact.

They rented *Jaws* from a kiosk in the grocery store while they were replenishing their snack larder and then went home.

Bob made a visit upstairs to see his little screw-top friend, and fell asleep on the couch somewhere between Quint's second and third barrel into the shark. The boys woke him during the credits and sent him upstairs.

This pattern proved prescient. They would go out at night, make big plans for the next day—"*if* we can get going early"— and everyone would take the oath. Bob would drink a lot, if not always too much, and would go to bed late—at least late for him. When the boys went to bed, he knew not. This gave him whatever morning there was left usually all to himself, and things kicked off at lunch at the earliest.

It was the morning after the show at Medieval Times— where Bob had an entire flagon of wine and Dean drove them home for a second time—that Bob gave the three boys a handful of cash and sent them off to the pier to get parasailing out of their system.

And then late in the afternoon, they were all up at Broadway on the Beach playing Dragon Lair Golf. The first few holes were calm enough—the flame-spouting dragon even made an appearance above them when they were on the fifth hole. But then Kyle had a few very bad shots, and Dean had a few very good ones, and things got tense. They got tenser when Dean wasn't content to just enjoy his own good fortune and began also enjoying his brother's rotten luck.

"Why don't you try aiming once," Dean sneered at his little brother on the fourteenth hole.

By this point, victory was out of the realm of mathematical possibility for Kyle. He took a swing at Dean's head with his short, green-handled club.

"Hey!" shouted Dean, ducking, and he grabbed the club after it missed him. He paused for just a moment, and then he used the club and Kyle's grip on it to push his little brother to the ground. Hard.

"Dean!" yelled Bob, turning around just in time to catch the shove. "Don't be such a jerk!"

Dean looked straight at his dad, and without breaking his gaze, flung Kyle's club out to just about dead center of the water hazard. There was a small splash as it ricocheted off the concrete octopus and landed in the drink. The game was over.

The next day, Bob actually made arrangements and signed them all up for something: surfboard lessons. They showed up at the Garden City Pier at 2:00 p.m., the incoming tide co-operating with their late schedule. Surfing—or trying to surf—was fun, even though they were all terrible at it. It was neutral territory for everybody, and they had a great instructor, who had them all cheering each other on. It was Kyle, to his eternal gratitude, who was the first one to get up on the board and ride a wave.

Try as he might, Dean, the athlete in the group—the kid on the swim team—couldn't get the hang of it. He kept overcompensating and was strong enough to keep pitching himself off the surfboard. Ultimately, after even Bob had done the big deed—but before his temper gave out—there was Dean, standing tall above the waves, their master for all of about eight seconds.

It was a shame that the goodwill dissipated so quickly after they got home. Bob had already gone upstairs and begun communing with the distilled spirits when he heard a crash come up from below.

"What the hell is going on down there?" he hollered ahead of himself as he thundered down the stairs. He reached the little foyer at the bottom and rounded the corner. In the living room he saw pieces of a lamp lying on a coffee table, and he saw Dean on top of Mark, pounding away on him. Had Bob looked a little more closely, he would have seen the cut on Dean's forehead.

"Dean! Get off him!" Bob shouted.

Kyle used this distraction to shove his brother off of Mark, sending Dean's skull whacking against the floor. Rubbing his head, Dean jumped to his feet and escaped out the sliding glass door. He jogged down the walkway at a quick pace and went out to the beach.

"Get back here!" Bob screamed. He ran out of the house after him. Somewhat the worse for wear, he didn't catch Dean until they were both not far from the water's edge.

"Who do you think you are, mister?" said Bob, when he caught up with him.

Dean turned, his face crimson. "Who do you think *you* are?"

"I'm your father!" yelled Bob.

"You are when you're sober."

Now Bob's face was scarlet—half mad and half embarrassed. "Now you listen to—"

Dean cut him off. "No, you listen to me, Mr. Perfect. Why don't you go back inside and have yourself a nice big drink? I'm sick of you!"

The sneer on Dean's face was truly terrible and unrelenting. Bob was churning inside, unable to think, able only to be hurt. He felt tears coming to his eyes.

"You know what? I'm sick of you too!" He almost stammered getting it out. "I don't have to take this anymore." He was red in the face, emotions swirling together on the same sunburned palette. He blurted this out, and now there he was, a middle-aged man in a yellow bathing suit, upset but still trying to seem somehow in control. He had thrown the feather boa over his shoulder but now had no exit. *Back to the house and those other brats? Forget it!* Bob couldn't just stand there; he didn't want to hear Dean's next line. He let gravity take him down the beach and on toward the ocean. Looking straight ahead, he jogged off the sand and pounded out into the water.

It was about the stupidest thing he could have done. *I'll teach you! I'll—I'll—what?* But now he was out from the shore, out into the rough sea, and past the first breakers. The other boys had come out of the house and joined Dean, and they all stood there watching Bob. If they tried to say anything to him, he couldn't hear them over the surf. He didn't want to hear them, anyway; he was sick of the lot of them. *Now what?* Now nothing. *Why can't I just stay out here?* he thought to himself. *Talk among yourselves, boys! I've had it!* He strode into the waves as best he could, getting knocked about and knocked down.

The current got stronger. As he felt the sea manhandling him, it soon got all of his attention. He was out pretty far now, the water pounding at his chest. It was still light out, but late, so no one else was in the water. He couldn't hear the boys yelling from the beach. He felt so stupid.

The ocean was powerful, lifting him almost off of his feet with every surge, pulling at him, carrying him back with it. Now he was bobbing up and down off his toes. Another wave, and he was like a ballet dancer *en pointe*, the grains of sand streaming in jets beneath his feet, rushing out to sea between his toes and carrying him along with them. Now he couldn't touch the bottom.

Bob tried turning against the current, tried turning around. As he rotated his body back to face the shore, the next wave rolled him completely over the top of himself. He came up facing back out to sea. He thrashed his arms into the ocean, trying to dig against the rushing current. No use. He was still going out.

He flailed his arms overhead, shouting back at the shore. A wave filled his mouth with water, and he coughed most of it up, pushing blindly against the sea. He was helpless against the solid pull of the water. Suddenly, he was afraid. Bob tried not to panic, but the more helpless he felt, the more afraid he became. It was getting harder to keep his head clear of the water. His arms grew tired as he pulled and pulled to free himself from the grip of the ocean.

"Dad!" he barely heard, and then he was rolled under again. When he fought his way back up to the surface, there it was again: "Dad!" It was louder the second time. He twisted against the current's grasp, hoping to see where the voice was coming from. "Dad!"

This time as the swell lifted him, he could see Dean. His son was alternately waving his arm and pulling powerfully toward him. While Dean was still a few feet away, Bob was tumbled over again by a wave. As he struggled his way toward the surface, he felt an arm thread under his own and then across his chest. And then he felt a sharp yank upward, and his head broke free of the water.

"Dad." Dean's mouth was close to his father's ear. Bob was still thrashing, trying to move them both against the current. "Dad. We're in a riptide. We have to go out with it. We can't fight it." There was a look of terror on Bob's face. Dean held his dad close to him. "Relax. I've got you." Bob stopped wrestling against his son. "Dad, it's going to be okay."

Dean swam directly with the current, pulling them both along, making no effort to try and move back toward shore. He fell into a routine of long, slow strokes, expending just enough energy to keep both their heads above the water. They followed the current where it led, and the ocean was no longer rough with them.

At last they could feel the pull of the water weakening around and beneath them. Dean turned them slowly aside from this gentler stream, which was still heading out to sea. They moved for a while parallel to the shore. Bob could see Kyle and Mark watching them from land. They were waving, shouting something he couldn't hear, and following them down the beach. Exhausted, Bob leaned back onto the stronger body of his son. The sky was so peaceful over their heads. A bright-white seagull sliced by just in front of them. He was no longer afraid.

A Castle in Rouen

S<small>LAM</small>!

And that was that.

He was gone.

Richard had walked out the door after yet another trumped-up fight, leaving Susan standing in the middle of the room, wondering what had just happened. She knew the gist of the thing; overly dramatic scenes were his specialty. She even knew the basic script: "You're too clingy. You're too suspicious. You're too…" something. But to pull this on the third day of their vacation? To storm out after using the *D* word? This was new. They'd rented this same house at the beach in South Carolina for eighteen—or was it nineteen?—years. They'd seen the kids grow up here, but that apparently didn't matter anymore.

Richard made it clear that he didn't want her coming with him. "Stay here; it's paid for. I'll be out of the house by the time you get back." Not even the pretense of trying. Did he have his return ticket all along, even before they'd gotten there? That thought made her mad at first, but then after a while, so very sad.

The cab came and went. When he called for it, that's when she realized something serious was really happening. That's when she got panicky. He was leaving her the car. He wasn't coming back. And there she was. Alone.

The sun began to fade quickly. She'd had too much wine and too many cigarettes but no food. She just somehow found herself in bed at some point. Susan stared at the ceiling, not even able to think. The big red numbers on the digital alarm clock traced themselves across her face all night.

The next day was a fog day, a ghost day. Nothing registered. She sat the whole long day inside the house, frozen at the kitchen table. Sat watching families play together, sat observing couples walk along the shore, and saw some of them stop to share a kiss. It was especially tough looking at the older couples, the ones who had stuck it out and were holding hands still. It was those couples that made her cry.

The day after was little better.

But the day following that one was objectively beautiful. The numbness was wearing off. Susan didn't have any plans at this point, but she was thinking. She made herself some coffee and had an egg and half of an English muffin. Then she shooed herself out of the house, and after pausing for a long time on the walkway, she went down to the beach. Susan wandered toward the pier in the warm morning sun, taking her coffee with her. She cradled the cup in her hands, and she could feel the sun warming her neck, her back, her face.

She came across two little kids parked out on the beach on a mound of sand not far from the pier. They were pretty young—maybe eight and nine years old—probably a brother and sister a year apart. The sister was the older one, which usually is easier at the beginning. Still, they were young to be out there that early by themselves. No doubt there was another woman with a coffee cup on a balcony close by, watching them.

They were making a fort in the sand, lost in their own private kingdom. Susan stopped far enough away so as not to interfere, and watched them attempt to build this thing. It was an outrageous structure that, once it achieved any altitude at all, kept collapsing. The kids did this again and again, always with the same result. And when their little pile of sand yielded to gravity and returned to the horizontal, the pair would erupt into a loud, fake wail: "Oh, no! Oh, no!" they cried. And after every brief period of mourning, they would break out laughing hysterically, flinging themselves around on the sand in convulsions. Then sitting back up, they would start in building again. They returned to their little universe of sand, everything and everyone else a million miles away.

A thought struck Susan. She let the cup in her hands drop into one looped index finger as she headed back to the blue beach house. She was moving faster now than at any time since Richard left.

She recalled seeing something tucked way up under the wooden stairs that led up to the house. She remembered a five-gallon bucket with a small shovel sticking out of it. "What's all this crap?" Richard said when he saw it. "They should have thrown this junk away." But it was still there, right where she had thought. Two buckets, actually, one inside the other.

Susan corkscrewed them apart, and underneath the top bucket, in the space between the two of them, there was an odd collection of implements, all a little worse for their exposure to the elements. *What was that? A melon baller?* And there was a butter knife, and a spoon—even a rusty spatula—and a little red, plastic shovel. She didn't know the purpose of each of them individually, but she knew what they meant when they were all taken together. She left her coffee cup on the bottom back stair, picked up the buckets, and headed back out again to the beach. On second thought, she ducked back into the house just long enough to put on a swimsuit and a coat of sunscreen.

It was a Thursday. The last-day desperation of Friday had not yet set in, and there was ample room on the beach. Still lots of unsettled territory, free of umbrellas, blankets, kids. The ocean was receding, creating plenty of new real estate. She walked out past the debris line left by high tide and picked herself a plot of clean, dry sand.

Susan took the small shovel out of the top five-gallon bucket. *Why were there two buckets? So two people could work?* She began smoothing out a large field, using the back of the shovel like a trowel. She picked away at the debris until the interior of her square was spotless, then smoothed the area again until every line had been erased. She plunged her shovel into the surrounding sand and started filling up one of the pails. She heaped the sand into the pail until it was full, then scraped the shovel over the top of it, leveling it out just so. Susan lifted the big bucket and picking the spot she wanted, hoisted it and flipped it perfectly upside down. *Whew!* Carefully, slowly she raised the bucket straight up, but as she began to do so, sand ran out at the bottom. As she lifted the pail higher, the sand began to gush out. When the bucket was completely clear, all that remained was an indistinct pile of tan-colored sugar.

She flung the plastic pail down—mad, defeated—and plopped herself down before the formless mound. Dejected, she put her hand into the pile and brought it back, holding her closed fist in front of her and letting the particles of sand run out of the bottom of her hand like an hourglass. A little stream of crystals fell across her open thigh, tickling her, until her hand was completely empty. She spread open her palm and saw that barely a grain of sand remained sticking to it. She was still discouraged, but she was fascinated.

Susan looked out toward the ocean just as a particularly strong wave shot up the wide expanse of the beach. Retreating, it left the sand behind it dark—very dark. She leaned forward and stretched herself out like a cat, went up on all fours, and slunk the short distance to where the ocean had just been. She shoved her hand into the wet sand and drew it back out. Her hand was a shelly clump, sand sticking to every part of it. And then Susan looked up the beach at that second empty bucket.

She stood to her feet and went back to her work site. Susan again shoveled one empty bucket full of the pretty white sand. Now she took the other bucket and marched into the ocean, not stopping until the water was calf high. She swooped it down and filled the five-gallon pail with seawater. Up the beach she lumbered with her heavy, sloshing prize. She was back in front of the bucket full of sand. Slowly Susan poured the ocean water into it, until it finally bubbled up to the rim of the pail, full.

This sand was now as dark as the sand at the edge of the ocean. She grabbed the handle and lifted it—it was so much heavier now! Again, she picked her spot and flipped the bucket perfectly over. It was water that ran out from under the overturned pail now. She waited. Then she bent low and curled her fingers under the bucket's rim. It wouldn't budge. She gave it a little twist as she pulled a second time, and this time, the bucket released its grip. Now it came up ever so slowly. She guided it carefully until it cleared the top of the sand, and then she tossed it safely away. What remained was a perfect, smooth cylinder in the shape of an upside-down five-gallon bucket.

Susan was ecstatic.

She smoothed the area around this new shape, redistributing the remains of the sugary pile from her first try. A dark monolith now occupied a barren plain. It was the most perfect thing that she had ever seen.

She sat there looking at it for the longest time. She didn't touch it; she barely dared to approach it. And then it struck her that it seemed so solitary, so isolated in this vast area that Susan had cleared for it. It seemed so alone.

She got to her feet, brushing the sand from her blue swimsuit and from her legs. Back to the sea she headed, bucket in hand. She fetched more water, and set the filled bucket at the perimeter of her cleared plain while she filled the other empty pail with the light, dry sand. She poured her seawater into the bucket of sand a little more confidently now. Then she picked up the outrageously heavy bucket and hovered over her target, straining with her back to keep her feet out of the pristine space. Carefully she flipped it over, afraid of crashing it into that first, perfect tower. Up came the bucket, slowly—up, up, until it was off and clear of the top, and then she tossed it gingerly aside.

What remained was a twin, identical to the first shape in every way. Susan didn't stop to admire; she soldiered off to the ocean and back again, and soon there was a third pillar of sand. She was excited. One more time this whole cycle played out, and then there they were: four perfect towers of sand, formed with the same care and deliberation as the pyramids. Massive. Profound. Confident.

She examined the cache of tools that was in the bottom of the second bucket. They looked to have been gathered in a scavenger hunt. There was that small red-plastic shovel, a butter knife, a teaspoon, a fork, and a few other out-of-place items. Judging from the rust starting to form on them, the utensils looked to have been pinched from the silverware drawer in the house some time ago. *A basting brush? And that melon baller?* Baffling. Ridiculous.

Susan picked up the little melon baller first. Except for that bit of rust, it was identical to the one sitting in her drawer back home in Illinois. It was so out of place to have it here in her hand—here! She put it into her palm and wrapped her fingers around it, putting her thumb on the back of the little silver cup. Susan stretched out her arm toward that very first sand tower and drew her hand down the length of the dark sand form. Moving her hand just an inch over from this first line, she repeated the motion. There! A column appeared! She couldn't believe it. This simple column, this detailed, chiseled *column* wasn't there before. She'd made it. Susan looked at the tool still in her hand—this tool standing by for her instructions—and she smiled.

She again sat back on the sand, looking at those four great towers, her mind traveling far away. She got to her feet and walked in a slow circle around the outside of the unblemished compound. She reversed her course, stopping with her hands on her open hips. Gulliver.

She began.

She made more of those columns, growing sure of herself as she worked. Inspired, she spread out her collection of odd-ball tools as though they were a surgeon's. She selected the butter knife next. Starting at the top of a tower, she stuck just the tip of the knife into the sand. First vertically and then horizontally, she excavated out a little slice of sand pie. Again and again she repeated this, all the way down the front of the cylinder in a steep spiral, right to the base of the structure. *Stairs!*

Susan hunted up some scallop shell halves and pressed them carefully into the spaces above the stairs, turning them into balconies. Bringing some dry reeds from the dunes, she snapped pieces off each one until they were the exact length of her little finger. Susan turned them into a bridge leading from the outside world into her keep, stopping between the base of two of the towers. A handful of shell bits, painstakingly inserted to make vertical mosaic rectangles, became windows.

Susan worked out detail by detail. This tool, then that. *What can I do with this little red shovel?* She didn't notice the time going by. She worked on one tower and then another, standing back time and time again to see to it that each was the match of the other.

She had to pee; she really had to pee. Susan bounded back to the house and ducked inside. Deed done, she picked a couple slices of Swiss cheese out of the fridge, grabbed a cigarette and lit it. She strolled back out onto the walkway. And then her eyes caught sight of a troop of three young boys marching in formation, heading straight toward her creation. She bolted toward the stairs.

The boys couldn't hear her shouting just yet, not over the ocean. Besides, they were intent on their target. They were not coming to admire. The biggest of the three strode ahead of his peers. Standing in front of the West Keep, he brought his right leg up in preparation for a vicious stomp.

It was at that moment that Susan reached them. Although she had surprised the boy, he was now about to complete his mission. Susan shocked both herself and the kid by rushing forward and shoving him backward.

"What the hell do you think you're doing?" she screamed at the stunned boy.

He started to stammer something, but she was still yelling. He wanted no part of this crazy lady. He didn't need the rest of the lecture; he just needed to look in Susan's eyes to know what to do next. He ran. The other two kids shook off their openmouthed bewilderment and ran after him.

Susan had startled herself. She couldn't believe how absolutely angry she'd gotten. The intensity of it scared her, but it was equally exhilarating. Those kids weren't coming back—at least not while she was around. This little part of the beach was her kingdom. She walked back to the house to replace the cigarette she had flung in the dune. Then she sat on the edge of the walkway, her fanny on top of the small wood table that doubled as an umbrella stand at the top of the stairs. She sat and let the smoke float lazily upward as she looked out at her four towers, some fifty feet in front of her. There she perched, admiring, guarding, and smiling. She took her time with her cigarette; she was in no hurry. When it was done, she snuffed it out on the outside of the railing. No time for food now—still too much to do.

Each tower now got its parapet. Careful, sugar-cube-sized shapes coming into being, one by one, until they ringed the top and touched. It was a good thing that she didn't need any more water; the ocean was far away now.

Hour after hour, Susan worked. She did get hungry from time to time as the afternoon wore on, but it went away, and the hot sun helped to hold down her appetite. She took the time for another smoke-and-pee break and finished off what was left of a quart of Piggly Wiggly potato salad.

She was working on the grounds now. There was a little grove of sea-oat tops. On a scouting trip, she found a small dried crab claw. She placed it in a circle made of reeds near the drawbridge and pressed some shells around it to form a shield; it now became part of a coat of arms.

It was getting quite late in the afternoon. The tide had changed some time ago, and the ocean was reclaiming its territory. She had been at this all day, not that she'd really noticed. Little beach villages had flourished all about her, springing up with their umbrellas and chairs and glistening bodies, but they had all come and gone. Those boys never did return.

The moat was completed, and featured little shell-patterned alligators, their dark eyes and tails visible around the circumference of the towers. The grounds were all done. A seagull had unknowingly contributed a large white black-tipped banner.

Finished. Susan straightened up from her knees, brushing the sand off them this one last time. *Finished.* She gathered up her tools, cleaned them, and carefully laid them in the bottom of one of the five-gallon buckets. She lowered the other empty pail on top of them and picked up both by the bottommost handle. Susan pulled out the small shovel that she had driven into the sand nearby. She carried all of her equipment back to the walkway and then up it and into the house, leaving the buckets, tools, and shovel on the back porch.

Susan reemerged a few minutes later, drifting back down the walk, swaying a cigarette in her left hand, a large glass of red wine in her right. She stopped at the little table and again sat on it, dangling her legs, surveying her small realm from afar.

A family walked by—probably two families, as there were quite a few in the group. They lingered for the longest time at her castle, always careful to keep a respectful distance. One pointed at this feature, and another pointed at that. Susan felt proud.

Her cigarette now gone, she sipped at her wine and smiled. She decided to take one more personal tour before it got too dark—one more good look in the twilight. She sighed, thinking of how beautiful it would be to wake up—maybe right at dawn—and start a new day. She could already imagine herself looking out of her upstairs window in the morning and seeing her little dominion. And then the joy of coming back to it, coffee in hand, and feeling the hope in what she'd just done.

It was only when she reached the foot of the wooden stairs, wine glass still in hand, that Susan looked out at the glistening ocean and realized how quickly it was coming back in. The drop-off that made the water seem so far away had been filled back in by the sea. The ocean was advancing now across a low, flat plain. Just a little increase in the tide now wrestled yards back away from the beach.

Susan set her wine glass firmly down on the bottom stair and walked briskly out to her castle. As she crossed down from the dunes, she stepped on the debris line—the high tide water mark—and froze. She looked down at her feet, nestled in the foot-wide brush, and then she looked up and down the beach, her eyes following the line. She looked straight ahead at her castle, a dozen feet in front of that line. Her stomach clenched.

She ran back to the walkway stairs and sprinted up to the back porch of the house. In a moment she was hurrying back toward the beach, the small shovel in her hand.

Susan started digging a hole, which grew into a trench, directly in front of her castle. A real moat this time. She extended it far out on either side, curving the ditch up toward the dunes, her digging rapid and forceful. Susan was no longer scared. She was angry.

The pulse waves—those waves that surge up every seventh wave or so—are the ocean probing its way forward. Surfers count on them and wait for them. Every few waves, here comes that one big wave that reaches in that much farther, that runs up the beach that much longer, before retreating. These scout waves were starting to get very close. Susan made her moat deeper, longer.

A film of ocean twinkled across the open beach, reached her, and then bubbled into the sand. Several waves later, Susan watched a little rill of sea water spill down the face of her trench, barely reaching the bottom of it before being absorbed by its forward side.

Another couple of minutes, and a new wave made its way in and left a little pool behind at the bottom of the trench. Susan was still digging, but she was hitting water now. The sand was much heavier in her shovel. With the shovel still in the bottom of her moat, Susan watched the next advancing wave spill over the side and submerge the shovel's head. Then another wave came and filled the trench further, and part of the seaward side fell into it. Susan began to cry.

The next big wave raced up the beach over the half-filled ditch and broke through the outer courtyard, leaving behind a circle of wet sand not unlike a lake. Just about every wave was reaching the failed moat now. The rogue waves were making their ways into the keep, lapping the bases of the towers themselves. Without warning, the East Tower collapsed, a third of it sliding quietly down itself, carrying the parapet, the shell windows, and the shell balcony. Susan gasped. The drawbridge that had been so carefully constructed of reeds was floating loosely about the courtyard.

The sun had gone completely by now. The full moon was taking over, shimmering out across the waves in a silvery blanket.

Susan still had the shovel in her hands. She sighed, letting it drift down the side of her leg and hit the sand—the sand and the water at her feet. She carried the shovel quietly back to the stairs of the walkway and leaned it up against them. She picked up the glass of wine that she'd left on the bottom stair and calmly walked her way back to her little kingdom.

The moon had transformed the whole of it into something ancient, something that belonged to a time long, long ago. She watched as the West Tower joined the others and made its inevitable way back into the sea. Susan stood away from it, much higher up on the sand, watching from a distance. Moonlight sparkled on the surface of the wine in her glass. She looked out over the whole broad ocean. The waves in this larger aspect seemed so calm, so peaceful in their steady rhythm. The bright moon bathed her in light. A tear ran down her cheek, dropping into the dry sand at her feet. It left a brief, dark circle behind, and then disappeared.

She Sells Seashells

THIS BEACH TRIP WOULD BE TOM'S first as the dad. From the time that Tom had been five years old, every other year his father had loaded up the whole family and driven them down to Florida. Two weeks at a time, yanked out of school, pardoned by a note dispatched from his dad to the principal. Two weeks. It had to be at least that long, because it took two days to get down from New Jersey on those old two-lane, fast-food-free, pre-interstate roads, and then another two days to get back. Five times they did this, right up until Tom was fifteen and his parents finally divorced.

Tom had a lot riding on this trip. To be honest with himself, he was apprehensive. He wanted so badly to give his wife, Janie, and their very young children the kind of vacation he had always hoped he'd have when he was a kid. He wanted to give them the magic and awesomeness of the ocean without all the yelling and fighting. He'd never been to Surfside Beach, South Carolina. It wouldn't be Florida, but Florida wasn't Florida anymore. Not the Florida he'd encountered on one of those few times he did go back down there to visit his dad. Everything from that long-ago Florida was long gone, replaced by the bigger, the taller, and the more astronomically expensive. But Surfside Beach was advertised as "the Family Beach." Although Tom had never been there, just driving down the Highway 17 bypass felt familiar. It was as though that childhood Florida had been teleported seven hundred miles north up the coastline.

Janie had actually never been to the ocean, so the whole experience was new and exciting to her. She loved it, just as she loved being a mommy to their two little girls—six-year-old twins, Christine and Elizabeth—and to little Tommy Jr., all eighteen months of him. And Tom was proud. Proud of his family and proud of the accomplishment of being here, of being the man able to rent the nice place right on the ocean. It was a happy man who herded the kids and the luggage up the stairs and into the beautiful blue house.

Unfortunately for Tom's reverie, a thunderstorm moved in at just the same time. It was a big one, even by local standards. As they were unpacking, that friendly blue ocean they'd been driving alongside just a short while ago turned dark and green and angry. Perched up in their beach house on the pilings, they got a close look at the black clouds clawing their way low on the agitated sea, and at the fierce lightning, touching off up and down the long horizon. The thunder filled the house, making the little girls scream and the baby cry, and it made the walls shake. A big blue beach umbrella came cartwheeling down the sand, powered by the strong wind blowing sideways behind it. It took just a moment to somersault out of sight.

When you're six, after about an hour, you think a storm will last forever. After another hour, you can't remember that it ever wasn't raining. It didn't help that this squall was such a rough one, shoving its shoulders up against the sides of the house and rocking it, seemingly just to hear the little girls inside shriek. And the thunder was not that soft, faraway, rumbly stuff; it was the big firecracker-tossed-in-the-sewer kind, loud and breaking in through the windows. Janie was too busy soothing the children and trying to distract them to notice that Tom's mood was getting darker too. He was getting restless at being cooped up as the hours dragged on—mad and irritated by his own inability to do anything about it.

The thunderstorm eventually did end, not that by that time Tom or his exhausted family even knew it.

But the next morning the rain came back—nothing as dramatic, but rain is rain, and it kept them all locked inside the house. What they saw looking out their windows made it seem as though the house had been lifted off its stilts, picked up, and carried to a place altogether different than the one that they had pulled up to that previous afternoon. They could see that the wind and the storm had rearranged everything. The little estuary canal a few houses up from them that had emptied straight into the ocean now flowed in front of them, dawdling parallel to the sea for quite a way until it finally turned and ducked in. And that clean, postcard beach they had first seen was now all Jackson Pollock, streaked and dotted and swirled with seaweed and debris.

Janie and the girls were eager to get out and explore as soon as the weather would let them, but Tom could only see the wreckage. Janie reached out and touched his shoulder. Seeing the disappointment in his eyes, she said softly, "Hey, what's wrong?"

He jerked away from her hand without a sound. Far away he went. Years and years away, to a little rainy living room in Florida, watching two grownups shouting and screaming at each other, their three little kids crying on the pullout sofa.

The rain lingered around like an unwelcome stranger all through that day. The girls knew they couldn't go out, and they were whiny about it, kept from their big adventure by this stupid, stupid rain. Janie was busy looking after everyone, and Tom grew more and more sullen. Things just weren't going his way. This wasn't what he'd had in mind: two days already gone out of their barely seven. He paced around the small living room. Without the promised and expected big excitement, the twins started picking on each other and the baby for entertainment. Even Elizabeth, who would normally be humming some happy tune, was standing up to her sister for a change. They kept these minor squabbles going constantly in the background, finally getting from Janie the inevitable, if undesirable, attention they were seeking.

Little Tommy Jr. had a bad nap that lit the fuse for the rest of the afternoon. An hour after he got up, Janie heard yelling in the back bedroom off the main floor. She poked her head in to see Tommy with Christine's favorite doll, now decapitated, its head in one of his clumpy little hands and its body in the other. Christine was beside herself, while Elizabeth had pulled herself tightly into a neutral corner. Tom came into the cramped room just in time to see Christine pull Tommy's hair. Then, before the small boy had even gotten out his first wail, she slapped him across the face. Janie went for the baby, but Tom went straight at Christine.

"What's wrong with you?" he yelled at her. "He's only a baby!"

Christine stuttered, scared, but still too mad to give into it. "W-w-well, he killed m-m-my baby!"

Tom stopped moving toward the little girl. He was grasping for control of the situation. At a loss, he could only sputter, "That's stupid!"

Christine yelled right back at him, "You're stupid!" and ran past him as he grabbed at her and missed.

"Get back here!" Tom yelled in frustration. The little boy cried more loudly in Janie's arms, but Tom yelled it again and again. He yelled it until Christine was too afraid not to come. She returned slowly, standing at last—terrified—in front of him.

Tom leveled right at her. "You apologize to me, young lady, or you will get your mouth washed out with soap!"

"Tom…" Janie started, but her voice trailed off. She was afraid that she might raise tensions by trying to ease them.

Elizabeth was crying, her hands over her ears. "Quiet. Quiet," she was saying to herself. Janie carried Tommy Jr. out of the room, Elizabeth trailing closely behind her.

Tom relented. When he heard his name spoken in that way, he felt as though some stranger—not "Tom"—had lost his temper. Yet there was Christine standing in front of him; he was stuck with this now.

He was just about to apologize when Christine said in a very shaky voice, "I'm sorry, Daddy."

It was just what he had demanded a moment before, but now when he heard this, he felt ashamed. "That's okay, honey," he managed. And then, after a short pause he added, "I'm sorry about Baby Beautiful."

Christine was only glad that the incident was over. Janie came back into the room after pacing with the crying little boy, Elizabeth following with an arm wrapped around one of Janie's legs. They had missed the apologies, but Tommy Jr. was quieting down. Christine ran up to Janie's unclaimed leg, looking out from behind it at her dad.

Tom went out into the rain to pick up fast food. He was glad to go, oblivious to his green shirt getting soaked and sticking to him. He was relieved to be away from all the scrutiny and disappointment. They quietly ate what he brought back.

The rain did indeed stop during the night, the sand already dry by the next morning. The kids could hardly wait to explore. They actually ate their breakfast—and quickly—so that they could get out that door. At last, the ocean!

The beach was a wreck. For every unusual or interesting shell, there were two or three shingles. What was surprising to all of them was that the ocean was the same way. Here bobbed a beam, half submerged in the water, lying in wait for an unsuspecting boat as though it were an alligator. What looked like a stingray was a sheet of tar paper, snatched from someone's new roof and now gliding by in the current, just below the surface. It was a mess. Janie stood looking out at the sea with Tom standing glumly beside her. There would be no swimming today.

Before that even got to be an issue, the twins and the little boy had involved themselves in something that had come ashore. Judging from the looks of the three of them, it must have been petroleum-based. Apparently the texture of the goo was just right. Whether each child had experimented solely with themselves, or whether they had used each other as canvases, every one of them was a black-streaked mess.

Janie caught up one girl while Tom scooped up the other, along with the protesting toddler. This was, after all, the most fun Tommy Jr. had had in three days. The whole clan headed up the beach in a beeline for the bathtub. Janie warmed up the shower and tossed in the oily kids, along with the couple of bath toys they had brought with them. She slid shut the frosted tub door to try and contain the shambles. After a few minutes, she set down the plug on the shower, letting the tub fill up so she could work on each of them in earnest. She asked Tom to keep an eye on them while she hunted up more washcloths and some bubble soap.

It took three separate rounds of soapy bath water, but Janie got the kids back to something close to their previous condition. It was, as usual, Elizabeth who was done with all this nonsense first; she was ready to do something else. Christine and Tommy Jr. stayed behind, their two toys attacking each other amid the warm, sudsy mountain ranges in the bath. As she blotted Elizabeth dry, Janie pulled the plug on their little kingdom and turned the shower back on just enough to let the drain have the advantage. Christine and Tommy adapted, standing up like little sudsy snowmen and continuing their battle. Not the day they had intended, but at least it was peaceful now, and they had achieved what was always that secondary parental goal: they were back to where they had started.

Just as Janie was nestling Elizabeth into the couch with a picture book, they both heard Christine yell at the top of her lungs, followed by a scream from Tommy. Tom happened to be closest to the bathroom at this point. When he rushed in, he could only see Christine over the edge of the tub. She was squatting, her arms pumping up and down. Tom looked over the lip of the tub and saw that she was astride Tommy Jr., her hands fisted in the boy's hair, banging his head on the bottom of the tub. Tom took one look at the crying toddler and lost it. Christine stared up at Tom's approach and screamed, "He bit me!"

Tom grabbed the little girl roughly by the middle of her arm. He yanked her out of the tub so hard that her hip smashed into the frame of the sliding tub door. Christine screamed, startling Tom enough that she wrenched her arm free of him. She curled up, naked and soaking wet, in the corner of the little entrance hall just outside the bath. She was sobbing, and when she saw the anger still in Tom's eyes, she screamed, "I hate you!"

Tom was still so flustered that he yelled back, "Oh yeah? I hate you too!"

Janie's face was white as she looked at the two of them. She had already come in behind Tom and picked up little Tommy. He was wrapped in a towel and on her hip, and his loud crying reassured her that he was okay. But she was unsure about her husband and her daughter. Christine looked so helpless crouched there, exposed and dripping on the wood floor in the harshly lit corner. Tom stood there frozen, numb. He felt ashamed when he caught sight of the red welt on Christine's hip. The bruise was staring at him, accusing him. A sense of despair came over him. Janie grabbed a towel and draped it over Christine, who began to sob in a loud, broken moan. In silence, Tom went through the hallway door and down the stairs to the car, his head pounding.

He found himself driving, but he didn't know where. He thought about his dad—about all the times he'd been chased around by him, belt always in his father's hand. He thought about all the promises he'd made to himself about the kind of father he would be when it was finally his turn. This was not the first time that this had happened, that Tom had run away, leaving behind his family, puzzled and unhappy.

It was getting dark when he returned. He was oddly conscious of the sound of his own steps going up the wooden stairs. He moved slowly, trying to be as quiet as possible, trying to keep his footsteps from sounding loud or menacing. He opened the door that same way, saying "Hi" to no one in particular, but saying it very softly.

Janie and the kids were all in the living room, with some sort of silly music playing in the background. They all paused when he entered. Janie's eyes were so sad when she looked at him. The girls looked, but then looked away. Tommy Jr. held his arms up. "Daddy!" The uncritical joy in his little boy's voice just made Tom feel that much worse.

Before he even had a chance to sit down, Janie suggested that they go out to eat at Pirate's Cove, a seafood smorgasbord they'd seen advertised again and again on TV.

"Sure," Tom said quickly, and the whole family was soon in the car and headed out.

The place was certainly distinctive, with its two huge, dueling plastic swordfish out front—made up to look like pirates, of course. The inside seemed like a pirate theme park, but with food. There was a pirate miniature golf course out back, visible through the windows. All the holes were numbered with little signs with skulls and crossbones on them. Inside the restaurant, each "port-of-call" station had a different grouping of foods—plenty of every conceivable starch—with a different fish and pirate tableau perched on top of it. The lines at the actual seafood stations were very long, but it didn't matter; it was just the kind of silliness they all needed. The twins loved it. Tommy Jr. finally had enough food variety to keep him interested. There was no hope in orchestrating any kind of balanced meal, so Tom and Janie just gave in to it, hiking back and forth to the serving areas with whatever child wanted to try whatever new food next. Their small table was soon awash in only partially emptied dishes. As the feast progressed, Tom caught sight of Christine watching him from the other side of Janie's plate, but they didn't speak.

Now that the storm had passed, workmen and trucks had been on their beach all that afternoon. Some were hauling the trash away in blue plastic barrels, while others worked the bigger stuff into the bucket of a front loader. The town of Surfside Beach was not about to let something like nature disappoint the tourists. The tides had taken care of the ocean itself, relocating elsewhere the trash that had been drifting in it the day before. The final Disney touch came well before it was even light. A small platoon of tractors, dragging heavy rakes behind them, headlights blazing in front, marched up and down the beach, literally combing and re-combing the sand until anything that might offend was either raked off or buried deeply out of sight. The entire beach looked like a giant sand trap at some country club.

Tom, Janie, and all the kids tromped down to the beach the first thing that morning, sensing that at long last it would welcome them. There had been a little time yet for nature to do more of her own work after the Disney crew departed. Tom was the first to notice all the holes going straight down into the sand and disappearing out of sight. They were smooth and symmetrical at the surface, like the bell of a trumpet, but ranging in size from only about an inch across to three or even four inches in diameter.

Christine noticed them too. "Daddy, what are those?" she asked. Her happy tone surprised him. After yesterday, he thought she might never talk to him again. There was no fear in her eyes, only curiosity. He bent down to her level.

"They're crab holes, honey."

"How come they're different sizes?"

"Because some crabs are small, and some crabs are big."

This was fascinating to her. He could see her making little silent computations as she looked at the different-sized burrows. They took a patrol down the beach together. He was glad she was talking to him this morning. In fact, he was grateful. His gratitude made him very attentive to her constant questions. Tom found himself making up all sorts of facts about crabs and crab families, crab schools, and crab birthday parties. Anything. Anything she might want to know, he explained to her, just for her to see him as the smart daddy again.

After they'd gone quite a way down the beach—the crab holes growing less frequent and finally vanishing from the topography—they saw an odd, dark clump. It was something that must have been just barely out of the reach of the big beach rakes. When they got right up to it, they saw that it was a mound of tiny fish, each one not even an inch in length. The small school must have crowded into a tidal pool during the storm and then been abandoned there when the ocean retreated. The little fish were just starting to dry out. Rather than let Christine focus on the demise of this ill-fated pod, Tom said brightly, "This sure is lucky for those crabs!"

His gambit worked. Christine turned slowly away from staring at the dead fish to look up at her dad. "Is this what crabs eat, Daddy?"

"Oh, this is their *favorite* food," he said, underscoring the word "favorite" to convey just how thoughtful the little fish had been to strand themselves there.

"But how will the crabs find them from way back over there?" she asked, pointing down the beach the way that they had come.

"Oh, they don't need to *see* them," he said, reassuringly. "They can *smell* them." (*Surely that really is the case*, he thought, trying to convince himself.)

She paused for just a moment and then asked, "But what if the wind doesn't blow? Or it blows so hard that the crabs *can't* smell the fishes?"

The pause that he took to consider how to address these two opposites was just enough to let Christine have another thought.

"No, Daddy," she said decidedly, "it's their favorite food. The crabs must be very hungry after all that raining. Maybe they're even too weak to come out of their holes," she said with concern. "We have to help them. We have to take the fish to them."

That was much too logical, which was the problem. Tom had always been proud of Christine's reasoning skills, and now he had been taken hostage by them. He looked all the way back they had come, and his mind began calculating how many holes there must be. He couldn't even see down the beach to the end of them. And then there was this big, stinky pile of fish. But with a smile on his face, he asked Christine very earnestly, "What should we do?"

She was earnest too—too earnest to smile right now. She was thinking this out her own way. "You pick up the fish and come with me."

He nodded quite obediently. "Okay" was all he said. He was all hers. He bent down on both knees and plunged both of his hands as far underneath the slimy mess as he could. He wasn't thinking about the rotting fish getting under his fingernails; he was only thinking about how special it was that she was giving him this chance to redeem himself. It could just as well have been cat poop.

Once he was fully provisioned, fish falling over the tops of both hands, he stood up and again said, "Okay," indicating that he was awaiting her orders.

"Let's get started" was all Christine said, and she turned and headed down the beach.

It wasn't far before the crab holes began appearing again. At the very first one she caught sight of, she stopped and turned to him. "Here, Daddy," she said, by way of direction. She motioned him to bend lower, and as he stooped down to her height, her tiny fingers plucked a tiny fish off the top of the pile he was carrying. She bent down and carefully placed the fish at the edge of the crab hole, the head of the little creature facing in, as though it might just decide on its own to swim down the hole.

That's *one*, he thought, laughing to himself, but he kept the very serious look on his face.

Christine moved to the next hole and repeated the process precisely. And again. And again. And again, always depositing one little fish, positioning it to swim on in. And again. And again. And again. Tom's back was getting a sharp cramp in it from the stoop he had to adopt, but he didn't let on. He noticed as they continued making their rounds on this food for shut-ins that he could now begin to see the oily pool of fish volunteers starting to drain, the exposed joints of his fingers indicating the drop in supply. He observed also, that the crab holes were again getting further apart, as though the two of them were heading into the crab suburbs. Christine hadn't quite picked up on this yet, intent as she was with each individual hole, with supplying each potential beneficiary. Happily, the crab holes and the tiny fish petered out at the same time—a perfect little touch.

"I think we're leaving their neighborhood," Tom ventured.

Once she had lined up her little fish, Christine stopped and looked around at the whole of the beach for the first time since they'd started. "They have a very, very big family," she said.

"Yes" was all he said, still wanting to take his cues from her. But he was also thinking to himself, *Maybe I can get out of this duck-walk position, try and stand erect, and we can walk home and wash our hands.* But he kept his smile in place. *Surely, these little fish will be gone by tomorrow*, he thought to himself. *The ocean will get them in a couple of hours or so*, he guessed, noticing that the tide had already begun to reverse itself, and the ocean was beginning to make its return march up the beach. *Then Christine will think they've all gotten fed, and she'll be happy.* That thought made him happy. *And, hey, just maybe the crabs will come out at dusk and beat the tide and eat all these crazy fish.*

"Well, we better go see what Mommy's doing," he volunteered.

But Christine said "Here," nodding first to the few remaining fish in his hand, then gesturing to a rather large hole, perhaps the biggest of them all. "Put the rest of the fish by this big hole. Maybe he's the daddy or the king."

He brushed the rest of the fish out of his hands and into a rough circle outlining the hole. *I'd hate to stick my fingers down there*, he thought to himself. "Done," he said, first brushing his hands together and then rubbing a handful of sand between them to try and clean them off. Christine was wiping her hands on the front of her swimsuit. Noticing that, he said, "Come on, honey, let's go wash our hands off in the ocean." And they walked the long way down to the tide line and dipped their hands into the next arriving wave.

"Okay. Let's go, honey."

"No, Daddy. You go. I need to stay." He knew she wasn't asking permission; she meant she was going to stay.

"But the crabs will see you. They won't come out." He wanted to give her an excuse to go back up to the house and clean up and take a rest.

"Then I'll hide," she said. "But you're too big to hide, Daddy. And you're too loud." She said this without any hint of judgment. "You go home."

"Actually, honey, the crabs don't come out until the sun starts to set and it gets dark."

"They might come out early today."

For you, they just might, he thought. He wasn't getting anywhere trying to talk her out of it; her mind was made up. And he was wondering what had been going on all this time with Janie and Elizabeth and Tommy Jr. Janie must have her hands full. *Okay. Okay. Let's see. How about if I can get her to hide where I can see her from our walkway? I'll just sit up there and keep an eye on her.*

He said, "Okay, Christine. Daddy knows a good place where you can hide." And he took her little hand, still sticky from the saltwater, and they walked together back toward their house. He got her up over a low dune and had her lie down on the other side of it, lining up her head with the end of their walkway. "Now you have to be absolutely still," he said, thinking to himself, *As if that's possible.* "Don't move an inch if you want them to come out. Their lookouts will see you." She took it all in and nodded her understanding. Then she wriggled further down into position behind the top of the dune, her eyes just peering over its top, and became stone still.

Tom started back in a straight line toward the house, looking frequently over his shoulder, making certain that she was still in his line of sight. He was just about to the foot of their stairs when he saw Janie running out of the house with Tommy in her arms. She was waving frantically at him. He broke into a run and met her in the middle of the walkway.

"I can't find Elizabeth!" she said, out of breath. "I've looked everywhere!"

"Hang on to Tommy. Let me look," he said, sprinting past her down the wooden walk. "Keep an eye on Christine, would you, honey?" He pointed out to the little sentry until Janie saw her, too, and nodded.

Where could a six-year-old be? He went through every room, every closet on the small first floor, all the while calling out, "Elizabeth!" As he stopped at the top of the stairs to shout his daughter's name once more, he was standing next to the little window at the end of the upstairs hall. Out of the corner of his eye something caught his attention. Blonde hair and a little brightly colored dress bounced along through the small space between two houses far up the street. They disappeared in an instant. He froze. Another moment later, there they briefly were again, moving in between the next set of houses and that much further away.

"I see her!" Tom shouted out a back window to Janie. "I'll get her!" he yelled as he bounded down the steps and out their front door. "Don't worry, Janie! I've got her!" He didn't pause for a reply from Janie, who was holding Tommy and watching a little girl lying absolutely still behind a sand dune.

When he got across the parking lot and to the street, there was Elizabeth, way up the sidewalk, just a little dot more than halfway to the Holiday Inn at the end of the long street. This continuous sight of her was very reassuring. Tom jogged up to her, slowing as he got close, not wanting to frighten her. He felt so relieved. He was trying to think of what he might say to her.

"Hi, sweetie," he started. "Where are you going?" He certainly wondered that himself. Janie always said that Elizabeth was that child you're sometimes given who rarely causes you any real trouble. Elizabeth usually asked permission for just about anything she did. Tom realized that he'd always taken Elizabeth for granted in this way.

"I don't know, Daddy." She looked at him carefully. "I'm running away."

"Running away?" he asked, barely able to grasp that she'd actually said that. "Why, sweetie?"

Elizabeth looked very thoughtful, trying to choose the right words. "It's too noisy at our house," she said at last. And then softly, she added, "I just wanted to be somewhere quiet."

Tom looked at the little girl, caught off guard by her words, and by a strong swell of sympathy for her.

"Do you mind if I walk with you, honey?" He really wanted her to have the chance to give him permission.

That made her beam up at him. "That would be nice, Daddy," she said through her smile.

He took her little hand in his. It was just the two of them in the whole world. They walked in the pretty sunshine, accompanied by a gentle breeze. As they were now so close to the Holiday Inn, an idea occurred to him.

"Would you like to go into the hotel with me, honey?" he offered. "They might have a restaurant, and we could get a snack."

"Yes, Daddy." She paused and then said, "I might be a little hungry."

Elizabeth now had her dad all to herself; for once, there was no sharing him.

They walked in underneath the large white dome sheltering the entrance. There weren't too many people around in the middle of a beautiful beach day like this one. The desk clerk pointed to a sandwich shop on the other side of the lobby. Tom basked in the approving look that an elderly lady sitting on a couch in the reception area gave them as they walked by. The little café was completely deserted; they had the place to themselves. A woman seated them with a pair of menus, and then a different woman came out of the kitchen to ask them what they wanted. Tom was going to wave her off for the moment, but Elizabeth piped right up.

"Could I have a really big glass of orange juice, please?"

"Of course." The woman gave the little girl a big smile. "And you?" she asked Tom.

"Just coffee," he said. "Coffee would be great."

She left, and it was just the two of them again. Elizabeth picked up her pink cloth napkin from under its silverware and, touching it to her cheek, said, "This place is pretty, Daddy."

Tom couldn't believe that he'd been given the opportunity to make her happy for just the price of a glass of orange juice. The way she was smiling at him now, her feet kicking underneath the tablecloth, made him feel so incredibly blessed. No guilt, no remorse—just the blessing of being here at this very moment.

Too quickly, the waitress returned with a very tall glass of orange juice and a cup of coffee. When she set it in front of Elizabeth, the child took a sip and then asked thoughtfully, "May I have a straw, please?" Yes, a straw—that would make the orange juice special indeed.

In a moment, she had her straw. She pulled it out of its paper wrapper and dropped it into the already-tall glass, but the top of the straw was well above her lips. Elizabeth leaned forward to get a sip and pulled the plastic drinking straw toward her so that it would reach down to her mouth. As she did so, the glass came along with the stiff straw, stood for just a moment on its edge as though it were on tiptoes, spun on its axis, and dumped itself straight into the little girl's lap. The entire contents of the glass poured down the front of her pretty dress. Elizabeth was shocked at first, but her eyes quickly filled with tears. She looked at Tom, and in addition to her disappointment, he could also clearly see that she was afraid. "You're not mad at me, are you, Daddy?" she asked, apprehensively.

She was afraid of him. That look in her eyes sent him back to his childhood, shrinking away from his own dad. When the realization hit him, he was so ashamed that he had to keep himself from turning away from her. But this time, he didn't run away. His own eyes filled with tears. He leaned forward and squeezed her small, sticky hand. "No, sweetie. Not at all. Not a bit in the world." And he brushed a sad tear from her cheek with the back of his hand. "I love you so much. It's all going to be okay."

Of course, now the waitress was nowhere to be seen. He didn't want to call attention to his daughter anyway; he didn't even want to take the chance that she might feel embarrassed. He picked up the pink napkins at the two other place settings, and along with his own, made a ball of them and blotted up her soaked-through dress. His kind attention to her calmed her down. Elizabeth had finished crying by the time the woman did appear.

Tom took a ten-dollar bill out of his pocket and handed it to the waitress. He wanted most of all to distract her attention from Elizabeth. "Sorry about my mess." He pulled Elizabeth's chair out for her and took her by the hand. Leaving behind his full cup of coffee, he and his daughter walked out of the café and into the hotel lobby. He could see her sunny mood beginning to return. Tom looked down at his little girl, proud of her for no reason, grateful to her for a million reasons.

He put his big hand under her small chin to lift her face up to him. She smiled.

"Would you walk me home?" he asked.

The Sandbox

JONATHAN'S NEW BABY SISTER CAME AS quite a surprise. Jonathan was happy about her too—at first. But her arrival knocked him off the golden perch he had enjoyed all of his eleven years. Jonathan could tell by all the fuss and adulation that he wasn't special anymore—she was. He missed his dad. Of course they still saw each other all the time, but it wasn't the same. They both knew it.

Sneaking out of the house at night became Jonathan's form of silent protest. It was exciting, turning off the burglar alarm and going wherever he felt like. It made him nervous at times—especially sneaking back in—but he didn't feel guilty. He felt grown up.

So this year, when his family went on their annual trip to the beach, Jonathan took careful note of how quietly one of the heavy sliding glass doors downstairs moved—the one on the left. Barely a low rumble if you moved it slowly enough. And the "lock," such as it was, was just a sawn-off length of broomstick placed in the door track. Roll away that two-foot piece of wood, and you could be gone with no one the wiser.

That very first night, once the house got quiet, he let himself out. When he reached the beach, he had two choices. To the left—north—he could head toward Myrtle Beach, shining like the Emerald City, about nine miles up the strand from them. There was almost no one on the beach that way, and he could be alone. The other way—south—stretching around the coast down past Garden City, was Murrell's Inlet and the tail of the Grand Strand. The Surfside Beach pier was only half a mile away in that direction. Bright, in its own way, and so much nearer. There were always people hanging around the pier.

Jonathan didn't want to take too many chances this first night, so he chose solitude and walked north. It wasn't long before numberless constellations and a shimmering moon became all the peace and quiet and self-reflection he could take. He was uneasy out there in the dark by himself. It was already lonely enough back home. Restless, he turned and headed back to the rented house.

The next night he headed for the pier.

Jonathan may have been old enough to sneak out, but he was younger than anyone hanging around at this hour. Much younger than just about all of them. People were clumped together out on the sand under the bright pier lights. Some were up on the dunes, while others were in the shadows directly underneath the structure. As he walked up on this, Jonathan didn't feel particularly cool; he felt uncomfortable and out of place. He stopped directly under the pier, the walkway overhead, and watched the waves come in. The surf came straight at him, the crisscross tiers of the pilings framing the waves, amplifying them, concentrating them between the wooden beams. It was hypnotic.

Suddenly self-conscious, Jonathan began walking again and made a single orbit as far out on the perimeter of the crowd as he could. He made one bold pass up the middle and headed straight back to his house.

The whole family, grandparents included, went out on the pier the next day. Most of them got ice cream cones, working on them slowly as they strolled the length of the boardwalk between rows of fishermen. A warm breeze came off the ocean. The bright sun sparkled on the water below. *What a different place in the daylight*, Jonathan thought. He wanted to hang around longer, but "Lilly needs her nap," they told him. He petitioned his dad. "I'm old enough to walk back to the house on my own." Dad shook his finger at him. "Jonathan, don't argue. We're all going. Now come on!"

Fine, Jonathan thought. *But you can't tell me what to do when you're asleep.*

That night, Jonathan was back under the pier. This time his plan was just to stand, just to *be there*, and not chicken out. He'd stand around, and if anybody got too close, he'd go stand someplace else. No eye contact, no talking to anybody—just stand and watch and try not to stick out.

He noticed a group of about three or four boys clustered around one of the pilings, barely out of reach of the bright rays overhead. The klieg lights on the pier bounced enough light off the sand that the lower halves of their bodies were lit, but their faces were in the dark.

Jonathan started over in their direction. He could see as he got closer that there were four boys, all older and bigger than him, though not by as much as most of the other people hanging out.

As he approached, Jonathan tried to walk in whatever type of walk he thought would make him appear confident, self-assured. He stopped at the piling that was directly opposite from these boys and slouched against it, making a point of facing away from them. He craned his head in their direction, trying to make out what they were saying. He heard "Brian" and "Sam" a couple of times, and "Tim" once, but the name he heard spoken most often was "Joey."

After a few minutes, the four boys' conversation started dying down, first one voice, and then another, dropping out. It was quiet under there now; Jonathan could only hear the buzz of the people out on the lit part of the beach. Except for the surf, silence. He thought about moving, but instead he tried to listen harder, curving his body toward the other piling. As soon as he did this, he was aware of someone circling around behind him. One of the bigger, older boys passed through the light—blond hair, stocky—and then back into darkness. He stopped directly in front of Jonathan. One at a time, the other three boys came and positioned themselves behind their leader.

"What's so interesting?"

Jonathan didn't make a sound. The older boy lowered himself a little and got directly in Jonathan's face.

"I said, what's so interesting?"

"Nothing," Jonathan said, still not looking at him.

"Oh," the boy said, turning around to glance at the other boys for effect. "So we're not interesting?" It worked; his friends snickered.

"No. I-I-I didn't mean anything," said Jonathan. He wished he hadn't stammered.

"What's your name?"

"Jonathan."

"You're not from here. Where are you from?"

"Maryland. Towson, Maryland."

"Towson, Maryland," the boy repeated in a mocking tone. Then, more seriously, he asked, "Are your folks rich?"

"I don't think so."

"You don't think so? Yeah, right. Another rich tourist." he snorted. "Well, Jonathan from Townson, Maryland, I'm Joey. This is Brian, Tim, and Sam," he pointed. "And we live here. That means you're in our territory, and you were spying on us." There was menace in his voice.

Jonathan looked at the boys and then out at the people sitting on the beach in the light. Joey guessed what he was thinking.

"You try to run, you try to yell, and we'll make you wish you hadn't, understand?" This came with more of a snarl. "Now let's get moving." When he said this, the other boys maneuvered themselves between Jonathan and the people behind them.

"Time to go," Brian said.

Jonathan hesitated. Joey took a step forward and abruptly shoved him at the shoulders. The move sent Jonathan's head whipping back so that it cracked against the wood pillar, loud enough to make a noise and hard enough to hurt. After that, he followed them without a word.

Jonathan felt sick to his stomach as they walked in a pack down the beach, away from the pier lights, farther and farther away from his house. The back of his head was still stinging from its collision with the piling. This was scary, like he was in a movie. *This is what I get for sneaking out.* He sure didn't feel grown up anymore.

When it was about as dark as it was going to get, Joey stopped, and everyone stopped.

"Okay," Joey said. "Walk out into the water." He gestured at Jonathan. "Get going."

"What?" said Jonathan. He stared at the ocean, stretching out into blackness.

"You heard me," said Joey. "I told you to walk out there—up to your waist." Taking a step closer to Jonathan, he said, "You're gonna go out there, one way or another." The other boys tightened into a circle around him.

Jonathan couldn't think. He was too scared to think. He just wanted to get away from these guys. *Okay, okay*, he thought to himself. *Just do it. Get it over with*. And he stepped down the beach and into the water. It was warm, but it was inky black, and at low tide it was shallow for quite a distance. When Jonathan got to just over his knees, he stopped. The four boys had all come down to the water's edge.

"What're you waiting for?" Joey said.

"My phone," Jonathan said, patting his pocket.

"Easy," said Joey. "Throw it to me."

Jonathan brought the phone carefully out of his pocket, a prized possession that he had only recently acquired. Water was already lapping up close to it. He peered at Joey, who was in an exaggerated catcher's stance.

"Come on. It's an easy toss. Hurry up!"

Jonathan bent forward and used an underhand throw to lob the phone in a long, slow arc straight to Joey—who put his outstretched hands into his pockets and stood up. The phone bounced off his hip and plunked into the ocean.

"Missed," said Joey.

Jonathan froze. He couldn't believe what he had just seen. That phone was the only thing of real value that he owned. What would he say to his dad? He had begged him for it and promised to guard it with his life. Now it was gone. He didn't move.

"I said, hurry up!" Joey yelled. "Or it's gonna be up to your neck, got it?"

Startled, Jonathan acknowledged him with a nod and turned to the black night. He hesitated, and then began to move farther and farther out into the dark.

"I think I saw this on *Shark Week!*" Tim yelled. All of them, even Joey, cracked up.

"Hey, is that a fin?" Sam shouted. "Look out!"

Jonathan was up to his waist now. The shore seemed far away—*very* far. He knew there were sharks out there, and stingrays too. He'd seen photos of them and other fish on a bulletin board on the pier. *What else is out here?* The water was not at all cold, but he was shaking. He was on the edge of tears. He felt completely and utterly helpless, frightened of staying, frightened of going back to the boys on shore. He stood there, and after what seemed forever, he heard Joey yell, "Okay! Okay! That's it! Come on in."

Jonathan trudged ashore.

"Wet your pants?" Brian said, when Jonathan was back standing among them. The other boys laughed. All Jonathan could think about was not crying in front of them.

"Where're you staying?" asked Joey. "We're gonna walk you home."

Jonathan knew he couldn't outrun them. And he had to go home some time. He silently started up the beach. When they came back up to the pier and the scatterings of people on the sand, the boys closed ranks. They didn't need to; Jonathan was wet and embarrassed about it, and besides, it seemed that they were just about done with him.

Before too long, they were past the dunes and in front of the darkened beach house. They all went together to the bottom of the stairs that connected the walkway to the beach. Joey stepped in front. "Right on the ocean? I knew you were rich," he said, inspecting the house. "I wonder what *that* costs a week." He turned to Jonathan. "We're gonna go to the top of the stairs and stay there until you go in, so we know this place is really yours."

Jonathan started to move toward the stairs, but Joey blocked his path. "Before we let you go, tell me something. What time is everybody asleep in your house?"

"Not late," Jonathan said, just wanting to get this over. "They're all asleep by about ten or ten thirty."

Joey lowered his voice. "Listen. Tomorrow night you meet us at the bottom of these stairs at eleven o'clock, understand?" Jonathan gaped at him. "Now we know where you live. And if you're not back here at eleven tomorrow night, you better be ready to stay in that house until you go back to Maryland. We catch you outside, making your little sandcastles, we'll kick the crap out of you." Grabbing Jonathan by the arm and squeez-ing it, he said, "Got it?" He didn't let go of that arm, even when Jonathan nodded yes. "Say it," said Joey. "Say, 'I'll be here at eleven tomorrow.'"

Jonathan said those exact words very slowly, deliberately, wanting to make sure that the way he said them was the way that would get the boys to let him go.

"All right," said Joey. "It won't be bad if you come—only if you don't come." He pointed toward the house and raised his voice up to a mocking tone. "Have a good ni-ight!"

Jonathan walked softly up the stairs, with the boys follow-ing him to just below the level of the walkway. From there he walked on alone. After he slid open the door to the house, he looked back down the walkway. The boys were gone.

The next day, Jonathan was sleepy, cranky, and picking at his food. His baby sister was fussy, so it was easier for his parents to give their eldest plenty of leeway. That afforded Jonathan a type of privacy but nothing helpful. His mind was elsewhere, and his score at Gilligan's Island minigolf proved it. When it somehow came out that his new phone was gone, he covered up in the only way he could think of: by dragging everyone back to everywhere they'd been to search for the thing. The whole family ended up hunting for his now nonexistent phone. Jonathan hated this lying; he only hoped the fake search would put an end to the matter. Ultimately, he wore them all out and they called off the snipe hunt. Dad lost his temper.

"You promised you were going to take care of it! You haven't even had it for a month!"

He didn't know why, but Jonathan was mad at his dad for saying that. *Oh, yeah?* he wanted to yell back. *Well, you only got it for me because of that dumb baby!*

Jonathan spent the afternoon sitting at the end of their boardwalk by himself, picking again and again at a couple of large splinters.

Later, when the baby was napping and the grandparents were ensconced with their own daughter—and when he had calmed down—Dad went looking for Jonathan. He could see that his son was anxious, and that made him more direct than usual.

"What's wrong, buddy?"

"Nothing," the boy said, almost with a sneer.

His dad let that go by. "Is this about the phone?"

Jonathan thought about telling him the truth, about getting it over with, but then he realized that he'd be answering questions about slipping out, and he just couldn't bring himself to do it.

"Um, yeah. Yeah, Dad. I'm sorry I lost it." This partial admission seemed to satisfy his father, but it did little for him. His chance to come clean had disappeared.

"That's okay, buddy." Dad sighed. "Maybe losing it will be a good lesson. It'll be a while before you get another one."

"I know."

His dad rubbed the top of his head and got up and left Jonathan sitting there alone.

When night came, Jonathan went into a panic.

But then eleven o'clock arrived, and he took the broomstick out of the door channel and slipped out to meet the boys, plodding slowly down the walkway to put himself back into their hands. He was sure of Joey's threat: *If you don't come, it will be worse.*

At the end of the boardwalk, he looked down the stairs—and there they all were. They were laughing quietly among themselves. Joey said, "Hi" with a camaraderie that threw Jonathan off guard. They walked as a group down the beach toward the pier, the four other boys making small talk, and in no hurry. Jonathan didn't exactly relax around them, but he did calm down. When they got to the beach below the pier, Joey said, "Let's go up to the Strip."

The Strip was a small string of overly lit shops and eateries that lined the walkway leading out onto the pier itself. Burgers, beer, and beachwear. During the summer they did as much business at night as they did in the daytime. A couple of the stores were so little that on holiday weekends, the only way you could get in was if somebody else came out.

The boys stopped at the foot of the broad wooden ramp leading up from the beach. Now Joey turned and put himself at direct eye level with Jonathan. "Here's the thing. We're gonna go in that store up there, the one on the left." He pointed to the beach store called Surf City. "That one," he said, making sure that Jonathan followed where he was pointing. "I'm gonna pick myself out a real sweet pair of board shorts, and you're gonna steal them for me."

What? Jonathan stiffened.

Joey said, very sharply, "You're gonna do it." He grabbed Jonathan's arm and twisted, causing the smaller boy to buckle in pain. "Listen, rich boy. Your parents can afford them, but my mom can't." Then, loosening his grip he said lightly, "Don't worry. You have the easy part. We make a scene, and you just grab the shorts and get out of there." He paused and then said, almost reassuringly, "Just to be safe, go all the way back up the beach, back to your place. We'll meet you."

Jonathan couldn't move.

"C'mon, I said!" Joey snapped. "Just make sure you know which ones I want. When you're sure, nod at me." And with Joey glaring at him, Jonathan nodded. The four boys herded him up the ramp.

Bright lights in the storefront illuminated beach towels displayed like medieval tapestries. One towel had a beer logo with four overinflated bodies in bikinis laying across it. One towel was a one-hundred-dollar bill. And one pictured a human skeleton surfing on the back of a skeleton shark. A lighted sign read, "Open til midnight."

There were a couple of people milling about inside. A small, middle-aged man sat on a stool behind the counter, right next to the cash register. His eyes locked on the boys as soon as they entered. The five of them walked through the narrow aisles, with Joey leading the way, and stopped under a poster of a skateboarding Tony Hawk that was hanging over two racks in the corner. He brushed his hand through the rack of shorts and then stopped and pulled out a black-and-white pair festooned with skulls. He stared straight at Jonathan and held his gaze until Jonathan nodded. The other three boys had gone over to the opposite end of the store, and now Joey sauntered over to join them. Once he got there, Brian and

Tim started yelling at each other. Sam got in the act too. Then Brian shoved Tim into a rack of swim goggles.

"Hey! Hey!" shouted the guy at the register. He hopped off his stool. When he did that, the two boys started shoving each other harder. Joey glared at Jonathan and nodded deliberately.

Jonathan's forehead was soaked with sweat. He walked over to the rack and grabbed a pair of shorts, stuffing them into the front of his own pants. As he yanked them loose, the little plastic hanger shot up and then clattered to the tile floor. The shopkeeper glanced over his shoulder toward the sound and stared Jonathan right in the eyes. At that moment, Joey shoved Brian into the guy full-force. Jonathan took off.

As he hurried away from the door, he could hear the store guy yelling, "Out! Out! Get the hell out of my store!" Jonathan was so weak from fear, so wobbly, that he almost tumbled down the wooden ramp headfirst. He grabbed the railing to keep himself upright. Once down to the beach, his walk was so stilted and awkward that people stared at him. He kept going and going, only wanting to be home.

When he got to the foot of his own walkway, he was all by himself. The house was completely dark. The board shorts were still tucked inside his pants. He was afraid to look at them, but then he was struck with the fear that he might have grabbed the wrong pair. Now he was scared not to look at them; he had to know before Joey did. Slowly, with his thumb and index finger, he stuck his hand into his pants and pinched at the other fabric. He pulled and pulled, until he saw the comforting appearance of a skull. Relieved, he yanked the whole thing out. He peered at the shorts as though they were from another galaxy. They were much bigger then what he wore. And there was the tag: sixty dollars. *Wow.*

He looked at that tag, fingering it. *Sixty dollars*, he thought. And then his dad came to mind. He would be so disappointed. *I'm a thief.*

Jonathan heard muffled voices, and then all four boys came into view. Tim had a torn pocket hanging down the front of his shirt. "Thanks," he said, looking at Brian and flipping the fabric back and forth with two fingers.

Joey stopped when he caught sight of the pants in Jonathan's hands. "For me?" he said, snatching them away. "Nice." He examined them in the dim light, then lifted his head and said to Jonathan, "I bet you never stole anything in your life. All you have to do is ask and it's yours."

What do you know? Jonathan thought, mad enough to almost say it.

"Okay. Tomorrow night," Joey said. "Same time. Right here. Night, night." And without waiting for Jonathan to answer, he and the other three turned and walked up over the dune, out of sight.

All day long the next day, Jonathan could still see that shopkeeper in his head, could see him staring straight at him. *He must know by now that I stole those pants*, he kept thinking. He was even more withdrawn than the day before. He felt a million miles away from his family. There was his baby sister in the center of a cooing circle, while he watched from a distance.

His dad tried to talk to him again. "This isn't really about the phone, is it, buddy? Something you want to tell me?"

There was an awkward silence between them. Jonathan tried to avoid his father's eyes. His fidgeting answered the question but didn't offer any explanation. He didn't want to talk about it. *What's the point?*

His dad was growing frustrated. "Listen," he said, "we only get this one week, once a year. Try and snap out of it, okay?"

Jonathan nodded his head. He knew he was letting go of another chance to get out of this mess, but he couldn't tell him about the board shorts—couldn't tell him about stealing.

The day dragged on and on, and now Jonathan didn't feel safe anywhere. What was he going to do? What would Joey have in mind next? All too soon, it was night again.

His mom thought that maybe he was sick. She hoped that it might help when he wanted to go to bed early.

He lay in the dark, listening to the dishes clank in the sink as they were rinsed and loaded in the dishwasher, and the low hum and the water splashing after they turned on the machine. Then he heard his parents coming upstairs. They cracked the door to his room, glanced in for a moment or so, and then checked in on his new sister and finally disappeared into their own room and closed the door. It was 10:23 p.m. All these weeks Jonathan had waited for it to get late, looking forward to sneaking out. When everyone was asleep, it was his time. Well, now it was his time, all right, and there was nothing he could do about it.

Jonathan was back at the end of the walkway at eleven. The boys were already there.

"Everybody asleep?" Joey asked him straight off.

"I think so," said Jonathan. "Just barely."

"Okay, Jonathan," said Joey. "Do this one and we're done."

"We're not going to the Strip, are we?" asked Jonathan nervously.

Joey laughed. "What do you think? Think they got your face on a wanted poster, Jesse James?" The other boys broke up over this. Then the three of them started bumping into Joey, egging him on.

"Just go in there," Joey said, nodding his head toward the house, "and bring back two hundred bucks. If you can't come up with the cash, bring stuff. Like a camera or a phone. Make sure it's something good."

Jonathan went numb. He couldn't even find a way to feel scared about it. He just stood there until Joey gave him a hard shove and said, "Go." Then he hung his head down and went up the wooden steps—a condemned man.

As Jonathan got closer to the dark house, a growing sense of nervousness snapped him back to reality. He set himself to do it, but his heart was pounding. In his fear, he started to think of what might satisfy Joey. Life was pretty loose at the beach, but most of the stuff people had stayed with them in their rooms. His mom usually kept her iPad in the kitchen, though, perched on a little stand. *Don't think about that yet*, he thought. *First get back in the house without waking anyone up.*

Jonathan squeezed himself through as narrow an opening in the sliding glass door as he could manage. He was inside. The house was completely quiet.

Now what? he thought to himself. Jonathan tiptoed into the kitchen. Scanning the counter, he could see that his mom's iPad wasn't propped up where it usually was. She must have taken it upstairs tonight. There was nothing on the big wooden dining table. He moved quietly back into the living room.

Puzzles, books, DVDs—the only thing of value in the room was the big flat-screen TV bolted to the wall.

Wait! He saw something lying by the recliner in the corner of the room. He went over to it and bent low. It was Grandpa's wallet. Jonathan recognized it immediately; how many times had the old man retrieved it from his pants and plucked out a dollar or two for him? It must have slipped out of his pocket during his after-dinner snooze. Jonathan's hands were shaking as he picked up the wallet and fanned the fading, Moroccan-leather billfold open. There must have been more than five hundred dollars in it, just in fifties! *Grandpa!*

Jonathan looked toward the walkway. In his mind, he could see the four older boys sitting on the steps, waiting for him. He thumbed through four of the fifty-dollar bills and started to pull them out of the wallet. He stopped. Then he turned his head and looked toward the dark, quiet stairs that led to his parents' bedroom.

No one could see him, but he was crying.

He put his grandpa's wallet on the kitchen counter and began feeling his way up the pitch-black stairway.

Climbing the stairs seemed to take forever, moving only inches at a time, careful not to make a sound.

Jonathan stood at the open door of his parents' bedroom. His mom was gently snoring. His dad was on the side of the bed closest to him. The boy crept in silently, on his hands and knees. He tugged at his father's pajama sleeve.

His dad began to wake up. Instinctively he reached to turn on his bedside light, but Jonathan stopped his hand. "Don't, please, Dad," he said in a soft voice. As the man struggled to get himself fully awake, Jonathan said, "Dad, I need to talk to you. I'm in trouble. I need to talk to you right now."

His dad nodded his understanding in the near darkness. "Okay. Okay," he whispered. He sat up and pushed himself out of bed. Jonathan took his hand and guided him down the hallway. At the bottom of the stairs, he again stopped the man from flipping the light switch. "No lights, okay?" His dad nodded in agreement, and they both sat down on the last step.

Jonathan couldn't speak. He wanted to say something. He had to say something now. He couldn't find a place to start.

His dad was alert now. His own eyes were getting used to the darkness. He saw the outline of his son and spoke. "Jonathan, you know how your mom and I always tell you that there's nothing you could do that would make us stop loving you? Don't you know that's still true tonight?"

That was it. The next moment, Jonathan was crying and telling his dad everything.

When Jonathan got to the part about stealing the two hundred dollars, his dad stiffened and looked past him toward the door leading back out to the beach. He stared for a while, and then turned back to look at Jonathan. "You know we're going to have to make it right with that guy at the store. We have to go back there tomorrow."

Jonathan gulped loud enough that his father heard it. His eyes were fixed straight down at the floor. He could feel himself sinking again.

His dad reached out and put his hand on his son's shoulder. "I said, '*we*.'"

Jonathan sighed, exhausted but relieved. His father's hand felt so comforting. He could have sat on that step with his dad all night.

"Come on," Dad said.

Slowly and deliberately, the man walked to the sliding glass door, the boy by his side. "Turn on the porch light, son."

Jonathan walked through the cracked-open door and onto the back porch. His hand felt along the wall until he found a switch. He flicked it.

The flash of light caught the quartet of boys sitting at the end of the walkway. They could see Jonathan plainly, standing in the bright light. They looked at each other, puzzled, but didn't move. The older boys were still staring at Jonathan when his dad walked out onto the porch and stood directly behind him.

Joey sprang to his feet. All four boys scrambled down the stairs, crashing against them as they did. They were visible again when their silhouettes fell on the sand, scurrying away in the glare of the moonlight. In another moment, father and son could see them no more.

Star Light, Star Bright

DAVID DIDN'T KNOW HOW TO EXPLAIN it, but now, almost a full year later, something still wasn't right. He tried to describe this new and awful emptiness, but it didn't make sense, least of all to him. His family and his friends decided he needed some time away; maybe a trip to the beach would help. Yes, that was it, they all thought; he had gone back to work at the observatory much too soon.

When that something had first gone wrong, David literally hadn't known what hit him. One moment he was sitting in a doctor's office, and the next, he was waking up in a bed in a silly back-ass-ward hospital gown. He was still woozy when the doctors came in to explain it to him. They didn't make any sense. "It's amazing that you made it. You're a miracle." *I'm a miracle*, he thought, and gave back in to sleep.

By the time Mary and their daughter, and then later, their son from Tampa, came, it had all been explained to him a dozen times. "Damn lucky," Bob from the university said when he came by and brought the flowers. "Damn lucky," he said again, shaking his head while surveying all those tubes.

But David, after all those years of studying the deaths of nebulae and galaxies and billions-of-years-old whatnots, had come face to face with his own expiration in that bed at Mount Saint Michael's Hospital. One moment he thought he was fine—that moment, that instant, nearly identical to the previous one in his long, lineal sequence—and then the very next instant, he had these people telling him how lucky he was to be alive. But he didn't feel lucky. He didn't feel lucky at all. After the initial shock, as he started to get just a little of his strength back, he could affect a sort of pasted-on I-feel-lucky-ness, but he didn't feel it. Instead, David now felt like one of his nebulae, certain of an uncertain process that would eventually extinguish him as well. In place of his presumed gratitude, what he really felt was a sense of resentment—resentment at having been awakened from a dream, a dream in which he, like his cosmos, went unquestionably on and on. Awakened, and then sent off to work at living out the end of his life, which, however many millions of light years away it might be, was surely coming and would come too soon. Only this time, it would be no surprise—no surprise at all.

Mary tried, but she didn't understand him anymore either. Mary, who had, for all these years, loved the man being rushed into surgery, was puzzled and troubled by the stranger who had been saved. Yet she was so genuinely grateful. After he was discharged, David pretended that tomorrow, that soon, it would all get better, that he would just snap out of it. He hated himself for being such a burden, such a worry. But when he couldn't shake it—when every morning he felt that same sense of emptiness—he began to think that there might be nothing to snap out of. He became more than annoyed by all the expectation of gratitude. Grateful for what? Eternity—or what now seemed to him to be the hoax of it—pounded in his ears like a celestial tinnitus, a ringing always, always there, waiting for him whenever it became too quiet. And it was always too quiet.

The plan was to get him away from the university, away from all the familiar things that seemed to so easily irritate him, and get him out to the beach, get him to some peaceful place. Mary would cook up a big family vacation, and all the kids would come.

The beach house was beautiful. Someone from the university had stayed in that very house the year before, and the rental outfit had just the week they wanted open. The house had plenty of room and was right on the beach. It was one of four facing the ocean out of a small complex of ten houses, with a pool as its nucleus. From their balcony on the northeast corner unit, they could see Myrtle Beach, nine miles away. The ocean-blue house with the sign reading Seas the Day above the carport was theirs for the week. David found that innocent name irritating.

Everybody made it in, which was great for Mary; now she had people she could talk to. This didn't seem to change much for David, though. When everybody went to the pool, he didn't go. "Okay if I stay behind?" he'd ask, and they'd all nod, just as he trained them to. The first day, he only left the house that night. He went to dinner, which he knew to be his minimum social requirement, and then he took a solitary walk on the beach—understandable for an astronomer—looking at "Daddy's stars," as his daughter Haley used to call them when she was a little girl.

Again, on the second night of their trip, David asked to go for a walk on his own. He saw his daughter and his son each touch Mary's arm as she stood there in the kitchen trying to smile her newly learned smile. "Dad's going to be fine," he heard their daughter say, as the glass door to the porch rolled shut behind him.

Once away from the fading warmth of the dunes, the wind blew a soft chill on past him and out to sea. A black night. It would have been a perfect night for his profession, but for the carnival of Myrtle Beach's lights—bright, garish colors. They were noisy to his eyes. But the ebony sky overhead absorbed their glare once he turned his back and started walking to the pier.

This beach getaway that was supposed to be relaxing him was having the opposite effect. When he had first tried going back to work at the observatory, he'd been obsessively drawn to the big scope, looking for something—looking, looking. And then he just stopped, just gave up and stayed in his office. Now that he was here, he was similarly attracted to the ocean, even though its enormity was having the same effect on him as the merciless stars. Both taunted him, reminding him that his presence in the universe was not required, thank you very much.

David went slowly down the empty beach; the clear night sky stretched above him, brilliant and precise. Millions of stars, millions. They all fell into what were, to him, their assigned categories, quadrants, and systems. He thought of how alive to him they had once been when he first met them, a boy just learning stories about heroes and gods immortalized in the heavens. Now that he knew so much more about them, it was as if they'd died. They were still in their millions and millions, but they were all dying. Just as he was dying—just as he almost had but still was. And how many of these were already dead, but David just didn't know it yet? How many were already dead, and would be discovered dead only after he was discovered dead? All of them sending out that one last distress signal before they simply ceased to be.

Caught in this realm of nothingness, the utterly empty space separating all these dying worlds from him now began to close in. The dark void of the night—this black vacuum overhead—descended and engulfed him. All the oxygen around him disappeared into the hungry darkness. Down it came, a cold, obsidian echo, until he was completely enveloped. He was alone in a vast, indifferent world. David bent over, his hands on his knees, sucking in what air he could.

There she was when he returned, waiting, as he knew she would be. Mary. She sat quietly in the corner of the family room, knitting something. They exchanged the basic pleasantries. He had to talk to her, had to tell her what he was going through, but how? So he didn't say anything. He went up the stairs in silence, knowing it would be time for bed soon.

In bed, they chatted about the weather, about the kids. It seemed safer, quieter there. And after thirty-five years together, they still kissed each other goodnight.

He missed her as soon as she turned out the light. And then, when she fell asleep, David felt really alone. The quiet darkness of the room magnified his fears, his dread. Everything in this small space became more and more pronounced—important, because these might be the very last things he would see on the very last night of his life. There was the clock, the sharp red numbers counting away the night, minute after minute disappearing. He was lying in a coffin, excruciatingly awake.

That next day an expedition was organized to go to Huntington Beach State Park. David went along, concerned about drawing everyone's attention to him if he didn't. It was a long, winding, two-lane road just off the highway that wandered alternately through pine forest and marsh before finding the seashore. Egrets, alligators, woodpeckers, turtles, ospreys. Later they went out to eat. Dinner was fine. The food was fine, and the grandchildren were fine; everybody was fine. Everyone was pleasant and chatting when they returned home.

The whole family wanted to take a late walk along the shore that night. This meant that staying home was David's only chance for solitude. They could see he was making an effort, so nobody minded when he slipped upstairs. He went out onto the back porch, the thick glass door riding the aluminum track and sealing him off from all the conviviality down below. He took a seat in an Adirondack chair. Soon all of the family was strolling along the walkway down below him, headed to the beach. And then it was quiet. He pulled his chair closer to the railing and scanned the sky.

The night was dark, still. The ocean calm too. A steady, even tide, providing silences. Far, far away the stars were sharp in the black sky. He heard a click from somewhere, and then a wispy plume, like the outer edge of an aurora borealis, drifted up on the right side of the quiet porch. It smelled pungent, sharp. Tobacco. He shifted his chair toward it, releasing a loud creak.

"Hey. Anybody up there?" came a woman's friendly voice from down below. It came from the first-level porch of the house next door.

He pulled back into his chair, but doing so sent out an even louder creak. Now feeling disclosed, David said slowly, "Hello." And fumbling for something else, added, "Nice night, isn't it?"

"Maybe it's nice outside. It sure isn't nice inside."

Before he had a chance to speak, she continued, "I don't know why they call it a 'vacation,' when it's just a different place to argue."

Her unguarded response startled him. The woman's voice sounded sad, and the words were not spoken sharply.

"Sorry," he said.

"Sorry for what?" she said quickly, now with a note of playfulness in her voice. He could hear her take a drag on the cigarette.

"Are you here for the week?" he asked. It was an unnecessary question; everyone was here for the week. But he wanted her to keep talking.

"Yeah," she answered. "We've got three families crammed into one house, and they can't even get along when they're in the same town. How many are you here with?"

"We have so many people, we don't know what to do," he said in a singsong and funny voice. *Where did that come from?* he thought. But it made her laugh. That laugh relaxed him and put him at ease. "Oh, we've got some grandkids, our kids, and my wife."

"Yeah, that's about what we've got. How old are yours?" She wanted to talk too.

"Well, mine are twenty-seven and thirty-two." And now he laughed. "But theirs are three, four, five, and—let me see—seven."

"You're funny," she said. Then she added thoughtfully, "You sounded younger."

Younger? he thought to himself. *When was the last time I felt 'younger'?*

So they talked. They talked about weather and restaurants at first, but then it was on to children, and finally, spouses. David could say nothing about Mary except how nice she was, and of course, patient. But he was vague about her, and why was he out here talking to Amy? Yes, Amy was her name, and by now she knew he was David. She demurred on her spouse, other than to say that they were "going through a rough patch." Neither of them wanted to go in. His house was empty, and the noise coming from her house meant that she wasn't missed. It was nice out here, just talking.

He told her about the stars that night. It started when Amy asked him what he did, and then she just kept on asking him questions. He was honored to have the chance to build out the whole sky for her, one constellation at a time. When she asked him things, basic kinds of questions—but big ones—he tried to take all the books and scientific journal articles and make sense of them for her. He delighted in hearing the sky get bigger and bigger to her, her voice excited and curious.

They never did see each other. Someone would have had to crane around a corner to accomplish that, but Amy made a game of it. "Stay a mystery," she said. "I could use a little mystery in my life."

Then David heard a voice come out from the house next door. "Hon? Hon?"

"Good night, David. I sure liked talking to you."

"Good night, Amy." And then he heard her screen door slam.

It was not much longer before he heard his family as they returning from their long stroll.

David was distracted but was more pleasant company the next day—enough so that everyone noticed. He had certainly slept better the night before. Mary seemed relieved, as though she was witnessing the first glimmer of an end to this very dark period. So that night, when he asked to go up to the porch by himself, they all thought it might be a part of what was starting to bring him back, and there was encouragement instead of objection.

He took up his post in the heavy white chair, looking at the sky just a little differently. He did not hope to expect—but was not surprised—when he heard the screen door slam in the house next door. Then he heard a lighter flick. He made a point of turning the Adirondack chair to make it creak.

"David?" It was Amy all right, her voice just a little apprehensive.

"Hi," he said quickly.

She laughed. "I sound like Romeo calling up to Juliet."

He laughed too. "How was your day?" he asked, because he wanted to know.

She talked about the different things they'd all done that day. But then she talked about her mother, who had died so young. And then about Bobby, her husband. David just listened. Her soft, womanly voice was like music coming from a radio, and then hanging in the night air—like listening to jazz while driving alone at night.

And he was flattered that she would talk to him like this, listen to him like this. He was surprised at how much it meant to him. He, in this terrible, lonely self-absorption of his, had lost touch with such basic connection. He'd become stuck in this constant sense of foreboding where no one could reach him and where he reminded himself of death all the time. Not now, though. Not listening to her beautiful, sweet, sad words riding up to him.

And then as Orion, eight hundred light-years away, slowly passed over the roofline, drifting silently from his massive hunting cudgel up to his right boot tip, David told Amy about what it was that had happened to him, about his experience of "waking up dead," as he called it, but only to himself.

Amy was shocked, as he knew she would be. But this was not followed by the usual transition to pity. She took it all in and then began asking him questions about it, about what he thought of the whole business now. David realized that she was not put off by his near-death experience; she was curious about him.

Amy kept listening to him, and David could feel himself relax, talking, just talking, as all of these feelings came out and out.

That voice came out of Amy's house again. "Honey?" it asked. "You still out there?"

She didn't answer. Instead, she whispered up to David, "Hey, I gotta go. I like you, David. You're so sweet."

"Good night, Amy." He wanted to say something; he just couldn't think what. "I like you, too," he blurted.

"Awww," she said, acknowledging him. And then a door slam, and she was gone.

David thought that when this pleasant sense of connection to Amy had passed, he might feel guilty about it. Guilty, not for flirting with Amy—he didn't know how to flirt—but because he was now having these feelings for her, feelings that he hadn't been having for a while, not even toward Mary. But the pleasantness when he thought of Amy did not pass, even as he sat alone on the porch and lingered there much longer.

And that night he slept.

The next day, at about midmorning, he stood with his coffee in his hand, just outside the back porch on the little landing that connected the house to the beach walkway. His eyes walked up the shore, strolling all the way up to Myrtle Beach.

Bam! The outside screen door on the neighboring house slammed, slammed, and then once more, each time releasing a scattering of small children in swimsuits, all wearing life vests. Out they came onto a walkway to the beach that was parallel to his own. He watched this children's crusade wobble down the narrow wooden walk, up a small flight of stairs, across a small stretch of landing, down another small flight of stairs, and then finally disappear off toward the beach. Each of the children brandished a brightly colored plastic toy of some sort. There was a pair of women hurrying through to catch the start of this procession, while one woman stayed at the end, encouraging stragglers.

This last woman was small and blond, and somewhere in her thirties. She had a pretty, if slightly puffy, face. Her body, the body of a young woman accustomed to finding nourishment by finishing the macaroni left by children, beautifully filled her red polka-dot swimsuit, which was just about a size too small and cut flatteringly low.

David noticed that she had her hand to her eyes, scanning his house. Of course it was Amy. She spotted him in the corner of his small porch and stopped, letting the little troop advance without her. She looked at him intently, taking a pose with one hand on her hip. Her whole body was saying, "Hmmm." He became self-conscious, standing up straight, and yes, pulling in his stomach a little. She took her hand from her face, and seeing him stare at her, she first looked around, then gave a deep curtsy. David's face turned red. He looked inside his own house, and seeing Mary talking to their daughter, answered with a slight bow. Amy blew him a kiss and then laughed a girlish laugh and scampered off to catch up to her charges.

It was no surprise to either of them, then, when they were both out on their porches that night.

"So, David, are you and me going to run off or what?" she said, laughing. "I mean, after today, I'll help you pack."

"Bad, huh?" he asked, in a voice of genuine concern.

"Tell me, why do all these people get together," Amy began, "when the only thing they know how to do is fight?" David heard her light her cigarette. "I mean, it's not like they even remember what they're arguing about, and yet it's like they never forget." She laughed a tired laugh. "Like that made any sense." She was quiet for a while, and he could hear her pace. "Come over to the corner, would you, David? I want to see you."

David leaned out of his chair to look at her. Then he stood up at the railing, and they just looked at each other silently, and for quite some time.

"Just a minute," Amy finally said, and then she disappeared into her house.

David tried to think, but he couldn't. These feelings were just happening, but now he was feeling guilty too—about Mary and about everyone. But that didn't stop him from craning his neck to see down to where Amy had just been. Then he heard the door directly opposite him slowly rumble open on the house across the way. And there was Amy, walking over toward him to the edge of her porch, just a dozen feet of night air separating them.

"Hey," Amy said softly.

"Hey," David said back in just that same tone of voice.

They were quiet again for a while, their hands on their respective wooden railings, just looking across the way at each other. Then Amy spoke.

"Hey, there's something I've got to find out. You have to do something for me."

"Sure," David said without hesitation.

"Meet me on the beach, David. I know it's crazy, but I gotta see you. Tomorrow we'll all be leaving. I know it sounds so corny, but tonight is all we have."

Tonight is all we have. That jarred David. *Tonight is all we have.*

"Meet me way over there," Amy said, pointing. "Right at the bottom, where those public stairs go out to the beach. Meet me on the other side of the dunes." There was urgency in her voice. "In ten minutes, okay?"

"Yes," David said. "Of course."

After moving the sliding glass door as quietly as she could, Amy slipped back into her house.

At once he felt excited and at the same time, afraid. He knew how serious this was. *What am I doing? What is she doing?* But he wanted to see Amy, and right now. And so he went downstairs, quietly passing by his family, and in a daze he found himself striding down the walkway that was the match to hers, hurrying to the spot she had pointed out, looking for her silhouette in the moonlight.

She was already there. He heard her call to him in an urgent whisper, "David! Over here!"

He was standing next to her in a moment. Impulsively, without even thinking about it, he hugged her. She was surprised, but she hugged him back, hugged him back hard. Then she relaxed her grip and said, "Well, this is great," with a sad irony in her voice. "I guess I just had to see what else I could screw up."

David was shaken by their touching, a touching that he'd initiated. It relaxed every tense part of him; it warmed him. He looked so tenderly at Amy. And then he took a deep breath and said, "I don't have any idea what's been happening to me this year, Amy. I've been miserable, and I've been making everybody else miserable. But I don't feel miserable now." He paused and looked out at the ocean. "Seven hundred million years ago, there wasn't an ocean here. In another million years, this spot could be a hundred feet underwater." He sighed. "And in ten thousand years, there won't be two of the molecules in our breath tonight that will still be in contact with one another."

She put a hand on her hip and looked at him curiously. "You think like that a lot, don't you?"

David shrugged his shoulders. "I have a lot of facts stuck in my head. I can't always tell when they're going to come out," he said sheepishly.

"Always the *professor*, huh?" she said, leaning heavily upon the word and then laughing.

He smiled back. Then he looked up into the night sky, and pointing, he exclaimed "Oh, look!" Amy tried to follow the line his outstretched arm made, but she didn't see anything in particular. David rolled each of his hands into a tube and put them one on top of the other, making them into a fake telescope. When Amy realized what he was doing, she slapped his arm, and they both laughed.

"Got time for a little walk?" she asked.

"Absolutely."

They strolled slowly down to the pier. The ocean at low tide gave them plenty of space, while the sound of the waves provided them with music. They talked about this and that, nothing special but the talking itself. David wasn't looking at the stars anymore; he was watching the moonlight in Amy's hair.

They lingered under the pier, taking half-hearted turns at starting back. The calm sea was at odds with the sounds of people walking above them.

Amy strolled out from under the soft light beneath the pier and into the beams of the klieg lights overhead. Like spotlights on a stage, they traced her form upon the sand. David came up alongside her, and there was only one shadow now. As they started back, the wind was in their faces—cool, but not cold. Amy nestled into David as they walked. He could feel his heart beating faster.

Then they were back to where they'd started. They were quiet, motionless, in sight of the stairway that led up to the brightly lit houses beyond the dunes.

Amy spoke first. "Hey, David, I don't know all those things about all those stars like you do," she said. "The only universe I really know is the one that I left up there back in that beach house." She sighed, looking in the direction of the lights that topped over the dune. "I don't know why I can't remember that." She looked at David for a long moment and brushed the hair from his head with the soft back of her hand.

"I-I-" she stammered and then sighed. "I wasn't just being a big ol' flirt. You mean something to me—something important."

David still felt the touch of her hand upon his face. He smiled and gently shook his head. "Flirt away. I've been the worst kind of dead for about a year now. I didn't see a way out of that until I started talking to you." David took a deep breath. "I just wanted to thank you."

"No, thank *you!*" Amy blurted out. "Getting to talk to somebody—getting to really talk and have somebody *really* listen—that meant so much to me, David. It's been like fresh air blowing down a coal mine."

David gave a little self-conscious laugh. "You're the first fresh air I've had in my life in a long, long time." He paused for a moment. "Felt good."

He'd been so aware of the effect that she'd been having on him that he hadn't noticed the effect he'd had on her in return. She had needed this same human touch that he'd needed, and he had been there to give it to her. He looked at Amy and sighed.

The shimmering light of the moon, tossing in the waves, sparkling everywhere, kept them quiet for a while. Amy rested her hand gently on David's shoulder.

"Before we get back to our universes," she said at last, "come on and kiss me. It's getting cold." She gave him a big, broad smile.

He smiled back. He cupped his hands gently over her ears, drawing her face up toward his. Her hair completely covered his hands, soft and liquid. He leaned forward and pressed his lips against hers. Her mouth was so warm, so hot.

"Hey," she said, giving him a playful little shove. "Hey." And she laughed and petted his face tenderly, taking just a small step back from him. "Here," she said sweetly, and she tucked her arm under his and turned them both toward the bright row of houses.

He let her lead him on; now he was leaning gently against her. The sound of the ocean, loud and rhythmic, began to fade as they reached the point between the bottoms of their respective walkways. David stood quietly, letting go of Amy's hand. Beyond the tops of their stairs, they could hear their noisy households. There was a shared sigh. David watched as Amy ascended her stairs, luminous as she climbed. His eyes followed her all the way to her house and past the screen door that she let close quietly behind her.

By himself in the dark, still night, David's gaze instinctively went heavenward. The Big Dipper—the very first constellation he had ever recognized—looked down on him, plain as day. He smiled up at it as to an old friend.

He heard voices coming up over the dune. David turned his head toward the warm lights of the house they came from—his house. At just that moment, he heard Mary's laughter rise above all the other voices within. The music of that voice called him. David slipped into a soft whistle and walked home.

Leviathan

TWENTY-SEVEN YEARS. TWENTY-SEVEN YEARS ROB HAD worked for that company—twenty-seven! And now he had a boss who was twenty-nine years old telling him, "We need to talk about the company's direction when you get back." A boss younger than one of his sons. Humiliating. What a way to start a vacation.

Well, he and Jeannie had been coming to Surfside Beach for almost that long. No need to spoil this for her. The kids and their kids would arrive just after they did. This was always really his trip, anyway; this week was his one chance a year to fish. This was his time, come what may. Maybe fishing would take his mind off things. The closer September came, the farther away the look in his eyes got as he sat at his desk. He looked forward all year long to standing on the shore with that rod in his hands.

Rob had caught a lot of fish in those twenty-odd years. Bluefish. Flounder. His share of sharks. An occasional sea trout. He even caught an ocean catfish once, an odd creature with the requisite whiskers and a dorsal fin like a ship's mast. Fall was the best; that's when the bait ran, the bluefish blitzed, and the big fish came in. Big fish. King mackerel. Big Spanish. Even cobia. Those really big fish that Rob had never caught. *Maybe this year.* And every trip, when he pulled his line in for the very last time, he was already thinking, *Maybe next year.*

He'd certainly had his share of close calls. In his desk drawer at work he kept a little shrine of pulled-straight hooks and chewed-through leaders. One September he lost *three* of those monsters. Each catastrophe had been slightly different. One fish simply stripped out so much line that when he tightened the drag on the reel to slow the high-pitched whine—*snap!*—the line went limp. Another ran away from him and got so far up the beach that the angle let the fish pull the hook free. And that third one jumped straight out in front of him like a missile shot from a submarine; it jumped, flung the hook from its mouth, and disappeared with a *take that* splash. Rob only had this one week, and it was always on-the-job training. A guy could go years without getting another bite like that, without getting another chance.

They took the short ride down to Surfside Beach, picked up the rental keys, and opened up the house. They still had a few hours until the rest of the tribe showed up. The house was the same as last year, but the owners had bought new dishes and glassware, and this year there was a new dining set. After changing out of their northern travel clothes and unpacking for the most part, Rob and Jeannie drove to the giant Walmart at the edge of town, just off Business 17. In their annual ritual, Jeannie took a cart and headed off to the left, toward the groceries, while Rob took a cart and headed straight toward sporting goods. Eighty bucks later, he was good to go. All he needed now was his daughter Becky—his lucky bait catcher—and she would be there soon.

This year carried a heightened importance, what with Rob not knowing what waited for him back home. He was more eager than ever to take his chance, to stand planted on the shore like a batter at the plate: ready, waiting. And yet—a batter hopes for just the right pitch, but there's always a pitch, *always* an incoming ball. In fishing, what the practitioner knows—and what the eager novice refuses to acknowledge—is that there must first be *fish*. The novice believes that his presence alone is the only essential. Alas, the practitioner concedes that while his presence is a precondition, it's the fish that are required.

Are there birds? What is the status of the tides? Fish about an hour either side of the tide change for the best results. Is there bait running? When the mullet school and swim in a thick carpet, heading always from north to south, there is bait for the fellow who knows how to catch it. Bait for the guy—or sometimes his patient wife or daughter—who can throw that cast net in perfect symmetry, who can make that weighted circle descend suddenly from above onto the teeming swell. When the time is right, you'll see those silver cigars so crowded in the sea that when the waves break, the mullet will speckle in a sheen as though fixed in a shower curtain. The birds are diving right in front of you, their beaks zeroing in as they plunge and reemerge, shake, and fly off clutching their meal. When the bluefish blitz, they form into a shimmering swarm that comes up from beneath, chasing the bait out of the sea for just that fraction of a second that the mullet hope will be enough to escape. The terrified bait will shoot out of the ocean in a surge from one end of a wave to the other, creating a zipper on the surface of the sea. When all this is going on, it's time to fish.

At the start of this particular trip, though, the weather just wouldn't cooperate. It was much too windy. It stirred up the water, the choppy waves shoving Rob's bait right back at him. He cast out trying to clear the tide break, but even a four-ounce sinker didn't make a difference—before it had much of a chance to attract anything, there was his line, come ashore like a plumb line, straight down the beach from where he stood.

What was one day? There was still plenty of time left. The bad fishing conditions gave him some time to explore places with the kids and grandkids.

Each morning Rob got up looking for things to change. He would stumble out of bed toward the curtains, looking out at the ocean and hoping to see that green light, the one that said "Go!" And then, finally, a day that was picture perfect. No wind, no rough water, and not many other fishermen.

Rob rushed out to set up his little field unit of buckets, rod and holder, net, and red-plastic tackle box. In just a minute, he was in the shallow surf, casting for bait. The mullet were moving in their little V-line pods, easy to see now that the surf was calm. He wasn't all that great with a net, always a little rusty at the start of a trip. But now he didn't need to be perfect; in just a couple of minutes, he had over a dozen of the silvery little fish. Becky could sleep in today; he was ready to go to work.

He did his part, but nothing. For hours he worked at it, changing bait from live to cut to using one of each on his double-hooked leader—but nothing.

The good weather came and stayed. Those last precious days, conditions remained ideal. He caught a few bluefish— some big ones—enough to take the edge off. And there were a couple of small sharks. Every fish has a different strike, a different fight. Bluefish give you a sharp pull and often a zig-zag run. If you're lucky enough to hook a sea trout, after that first bite, they may run in on you so that you think they're gone. Their mouths are so weak that you can't count them caught until they're out of the water and five feet up the beach. Flounder suck the bait, and you may not know that you have them on until they find the hook. And a shark, whatever its size, is like hooking onto the back of a pickup truck. They grab the bait and shoot straight out from you—all power and no grace—and if they scrape that line against their body, that coarse skin can sandpaper them free.

Rob tried not to think about work, but with the fishing action this slow, he couldn't help it. He was done being angry about it. Now he was worried that he might actually lose this job that he thought he hated. He was a little afraid.

So here was one last perfect day. Friday. This was it. They were driving back to Wisconsin in the morning. Out Rob went, determined as ever, and ready to do his part. He set up his camp again, and this time, the last time this year, he could care less about "optimal tide patterns"—he was here to stay.

Becky did her bit. She was out there soon after her dad was. Becky had been his fishing buddy since she was nine. She specialized in throwing the cast net and catching the mullet. She kept the job all the way through college. She tossed the net and filled him up a bucket full of bait, before heading back to the house to make breakfast for her kids.

About 10:00 a.m. or so, Jeannie came down, and you could see she had done this many times. Not so much a dutiful wife—more like a nurse in an asylum. She brought him a magnificent egg-and-cheese-and-toast contraption, all wrapped in a paper towel and accompanied by a really cold beer.

"How's it going?"

"A little slow."

They both knew that was code for "dead."

It was another couple of hours before she returned. In the meantime, he waded a little deeper than usual out into the ocean on one of his casts and jettisoned the beer. The kids made it down, one by one, to pay their respects. There was still some bait moving in the water, though now it was a little farther out. This time, Jeannie brought the spray sunscreen. Rob turned around like a rotisserie chicken, and she applied it in a fine mist.

"How's it going?"

"Slow."

"The kids want to go down to Garden City to eat at Fred's."

"Great," he answered, a little too quickly.

They'd been going to Fred's for just about all of those twenty-some years. Funny to think that now their kids could drive them.

"Can I take them?" The question was not so much to ask permission as it was to ask, "Are you going to be all right?"

"Sure. Sure." He was distracted, but he was clear. "Go."

"What can I get you before I go?"

"I'm fine. I'm fine. Get me something when you get back."

Jeannie leaned in and kissed off the sunscreen on the back of his neck. "We're all rooting for you."

"Okay. Thanks." As she headed up the beach toward the house he yelled after her, "Thanks!"

After Jeannie left, the sun got brighter and hotter and hotter. Without a wind, Rob was sweating, the sunscreen stinging at the corners of his eyes. Still no fish. Of the other guys who had shown up to fish, the fellow two rods up the beach from him now packed up and left. That left four of them: one older guy on his left, and two guys spread out down the beach on his right. In another hour, it was down to three.

It got later and later, and still no action. Rob was getting stingier with the fresh bait, sometimes substituting some shrimp he'd bought at the pier. The mullet were all but gone from the surf; he had to go hike back up the little brackish swash that emptied into the ocean to catch some. His boss would tell him that this was unproductive, that he had entered into a point of diminishing returns. His boss would see his continued efforts as a sign of inflexibility, of putting his own stubborn desires over those of the team.

Jeannie finally came back, another beer in hand, another sandwich wrapped in a paper towel. She was a little sheepish at having been gone so long. Rob hadn't noticed.

After the long day, the sun started to hunker down behind the roofs of the houses in back of him. Once the direct rays left, so did the sunbathers. A little exodus ensued as one small group and then another gathered up blankets and empties and put back on their flip-flops.

Now the guy on Rob's right packed it in; the old guy on his left had already gone. It was just Rob and one guy down past the swash. The pull of the surf on his legs as he trudged out to cast and walk back was starting to tire him. The soft, wet sand shifting under his feet was making them ache.

It was promenade time now. Families were all cleaned up and back together, either coming home from an early supper or getting ready to go out to a later one. The older men checked in with him to get the day's tally. On days when it was impressive, there were always more questions, queries about bait selection and technique. No extra questioning today.

His daughter Becky came down.

"Tough, huh?" she asked sympathetically.

"Slow."

"Anything?"

"Some big bites before lunch."

She smiled. As his fishing comrade, she knew the code.

They stood side by side, connected despite his frustration, gazing out over the ocean at absolutely nothing. Buddies.

Jeannie was back again, this time with some red wine in a coffee cup. Back at the house, she and the other kids had been ping-ponging restaurant names. But she took a long look at Rob, stroked the hair out of his eyes, and made the decision for all of them.

"I'm making spaghetti," she announced, as if it had been planned for days.

"Sounds great," Rob said gratefully, absentmindedly.

"Not too long," she said, dropping a little marker about the time.

"Not too long," he repeated in the same voice, now speaking as the last of the fishermen. The last guy had left, pulling in his line and chucking his leftover bait into the ocean. It was Rob, and Rob alone now.

He was surprised at himself—surprised that he'd stayed out the whole solid day. It had been years since he'd done something like that, but it had been years since everything seemed so confusing. His mind went back to his job and to his boss. What would it take to please the guy? *Do I have to be twenty-five again? Is that all that counts?* He knew he was still useful. Why didn't anybody else?

At least there was nothing confusing about fishing. He had been doing this for twenty-some years, as he would tell any interested passerby who might stop to get a fishing report. He changed baits from time to time, changed hook sizes, rigs; there was always some new gimmick at Big Jim's Bait and Tackle that he went for. But this—this did not change. Standing at the ocean's edge, waiting, hoping—this was always the same.

Becky hadn't left; she was still right there. She was tempted by the rowdy laughter of her siblings and her own kids back in the house, and she turned her head every now and then to catch the racket, but this was pretty special. One on one with anybody is always hard to pull off in a big family, especially a close one. And this was her dad.

Becky could tell something big was bothering him. But even when he was in a great mood, the fishing conversation went about the same. They had their own little dialect. She knew that he'd get around to letting her know what had him so gloomy.

They smiled at each other. "Can you hold this?" Rob said, gesturing with the pole. "I need to get some fresh water for the bait."

She asked anyway. "Want me to get it?"

"No, that's fine," he answered. "It'll just take me a second."

She knew the drill. She moved over to her dad and received the rod into both her hands. This was probably the thousandth time she'd done this.

Rob tipped out the spare bucket, turning the white sand underneath it temporarily dark, and headed down to the nearby water. Once the pail was full of seawater, he lugged it awkwardly back up the beach. As he poured the fresh, oxygen-rich water over his captives, Becky stomped her foot down on the sand.

"Whoa!"

Rob shot a look over at her, and watched the fishing rod arc itself into an inverted U shape.

"Whoa!" Becky yelled again, this time more apprehensively. A moment later she was dancing on the balls of her feet and being dragged down to the ocean, accelerating forward with the rod still firmly in her grasp. "Dad! Dad!" she shouted over her shoulder.

Rob dropped the bucket and ran to intercept her. He came up behind her in a sort of straightjacket embrace. They slowed down considerably, but the awkwardness of their stance still let them be jerked forward.

"Take it! Take it!" Becky pleaded.

Rob locked both of his arms onto the rod, and Becky slipped underneath them. The next jolt transferred directly to his shoulders and made him fold to absorb it.

This is big, whatever it is, he thought to himself. *Big.*

He put his fingers on the small triangle of plastic sitting on top of the reel and twisted it slowly counterclockwise, lessening the drag. At once, the fishing line whined out of the reel, and the rod eased into a less dramatic arc.

While relaxing the tension on the line kept the fish from breaking it, now it played off the spool quickly, like a kite shooting up into the sky. At this rate, it would play out down to that last knot on a barren reel. He would have to tighten the drag again before he ran out; there was no other choice. *Why don't I have heavier line on? This thing's going to snap it!* Clockwise went the small white triangle, and again the rod bowed down, and again Rob bent forward.

And then it stopped. Whatever it was just stopped way out there somewhere. There was no more pulling strong enough to strip line; there was no retreat. Man and unknown creature were frozen in place, as though eyeing each other through the surface of the sea.

The line loosened suddenly, causing Rob to stagger and almost lose his balance. The rod came straight back to attention, shedding all of its curve. The fish was running in toward him.

Frantically, he reeled the line in, faster and faster, to keep it free of any slack that would allow the fish to shudder its head and throw the hook.

It wasn't just Becky with him now. Her whoops had drawn a small crowd that was getting bigger as people walked up from all directions. The lights flipped on in the beach house, and Jeannie and all the kids came running down the walkway, Jeannie with a camera in her hand.

The fish—and a fish was what Rob wanted this to be, not a shark, not a ray, not a scuba diver—was moving down the beach now, headed toward the distant pier. As it moved, Rob moved, and the small crowd moved, too, with Rob as its nucleus. He had to keep this creature in front of him. He'd lost some big fish just this way. Too sharp of an angle, and the tail would slice the line. Even if it were a shark, there was that rubbing of the line against that harsh skin to avoid.

As the two of them fought, the sun flickered out in a burst of reds and brilliant oranges thrown overhead and spilled across the sand. Then it was gone.

The moon took over. Brighter and brighter it got, like a flashlight glistening over the waves and pointing straight at him.

Nobody left. Nobody would, as long as that line stayed taut and that rod stayed bent. There were maybe forty people around him now. Lots of them were talking, and a few were taking pictures, although some of those pictures might have had more to do with the way the moonlight was splashing out across the water.

"That's a shark," said an older guy who walked up to stand right beside him, trying to hitch onto Rob's fight. "Might as well cut it now," he said. "If it isn't a shark, it's a ray."

Rob looked at him in a most uninviting way.

Expanding on his self-appointed role, the old guy said, "There's a thousand-dollar fine for catching sharks on purpose."

Whatever it was out there, it was changing tactics. Rob felt it pull and turn and now head in the other direction back up the beach. Rob and his band of acolytes followed after it, as he tried to keep the line pointing straight in toward the beach. *Stay in front of him. Stay in front of him,* Rob kept repeating to himself.

The crowd—with the exception of the old guy, who was foisting himself off as a not-so-silent partner—kept a respectful distance, and fanned out in a semicircle, like they were in a Greek amphitheater.

Something changed. Now Rob was making five turns of the reel and losing only one turn back. The creature was beginning to give way. Rob kept his feet flat on the sand, holding a slight steady lean backward on the rod. It stalled. That sharp pull was gone. Now he was reeling in ten turns of the reel with only a half-hearted loss of one. And then there was no loss. It was tired. Rob was making headway. Whatever it was, it was giving up.

Slowly, his rival was being pulled toward him. Rob brought it in ever so gently, worried about the strength of his line. He'd held the creature to a draw thus far, but now he was fighting the ocean itself. As he brought whatever it was into shallower and shallower water, the tide tried to suck it back out, the sheer weight of the thing pulling on his thin line and again stripping it off. The dead weight of the thing was being tugged back out with the current and was creating more than enough tension at this point to snap his line—and Rob knew it.

He began to time his retrieve to match the tide. Retrieve. Pause. Retrieve. Pause. The creature moved through the biggest of the waves, but was still pretty far out there. In the bright moonlight, he could now see a dark shape moving into the shallower water. There was a splash. Was that a tail or a fin?

"Hey, remember, the fine could be a thousand bucks if that's a shark," the old character grumbled to Rob. "Not too late to cut that line."

But Rob wasn't listening. He felt that the animal had sort of run itself aground. Its weight was resting on a sandbar still about forty feet in front of him—too far to make it possible to grab him and haul him in, too far and too heavy for Rob's lighter line to just drag him. He was stuck.

Rob had enough tide and just enough depth of water left to try and work with. As the ocean swept by the beast, he pulled, getting it to move forward on the thin film of water underneath it. Again. Another wave. Again.

"It's a fish! It's a fish!" Becky screamed.

Once more, he surfed it over another sandbar. Then another one. And with one more wave and one last gentle tug, up onto the beach it came, the ocean now abandoning it completely.

It was a fish indeed.

His little gallery let up a cheer. There was applause. Out came all the cell phones, and Rob knelt obligingly beside the fish—Hemingway with his lion.

How huge it was! Not quite a man's length, but certainly a child's. It was lustrous, as the moonlight played over its large scales. Brown-speckled and shiny on the surface, like a trout, and pale white on its sizable belly. Its head was large, and the tail was like a whale's fluke turned sideways, with a cluster of four dots on the bottom part. Whatever it was, it was massive.

"Mister, that fish is illegal," the irritant beside him declared.

The man was staring at Rob, but Rob was not looking at him. "What?" Rob asked quietly, only partially turning his head toward him. He was entranced by this huge, shimmering creature.

"That's a red drum," the old guy said authoritatively.

"A what?" Now he had Rob's attention.

"A red drum." The guy said again. "Redfish. A spottail." He paused for effect. "Man, that fish is so far over the limit, it isn't even funny."

"There's a *too big*?" Rob asked, incredulous.

"Yep," the guy said, adding a vigorous nod. "And *that* bull drum is *double* too big!"

Rob looked at the fish, not the guy, and watched as its mouth gaped open, sucking the air. The body of the fish was heaving up and down on the shiny sand, the moonlight bouncing off its back.

Rob's shoulders had a mild, pleasant throb. He stooped down and lifted the fish up with both of his arms and then thrust it high over his head. He surprised himself, doing it. How heavy it was! He got another round of cheers, and now everyone was taking the same picture—the moonlight behind Rob framing him and the fish.

The unwanted buddy was next to him again. This time his tone was deferential. "Man, I've been fishing off of here for *thirty years*, and I've *never* seen anything like this. Not off the beach." He paused again, and then spoke in a lower tone. "But that fish is illegal."

Rob slowly, gently, lowered his trophy. The animal was exhausted; it barely wriggled in his arms. *I wonder how old you are*, Rob thought to himself. The big fish was still very much alive, the mouth sucking, the hard gills flaring in and out. It had thrown the hook from its jaw when it first came ashore. Rob took another good look at the animal. He turned to the old fellow and said, "Nothing illegal about this fish."

He walked away from them all with the fish cradled in his arms. In several steps, he was back in the surf and out past the shallow sandbars, in open water up over his knees. Rob lowered this living thing back into the water as though he were placing a sleeping baby back into a crib. Back and forth he rocked the fish, moving his own body, his motion making its tail move side to side in response. Side to side they went, patient and at peace, just the two of them out there—everyone else left behind on the beach, far, far away.

The tail woke up first, a little splash that sent drops of water up Rob's chest. Another thrash, and this time the body moved with the tail. Nothing forceful, but full head-to-tail undulation. Man and fish were making the same motions, until at last, the fish's rhythms took over from Rob's. Suddenly, with a deep stroke, the fish lifted itself up and out of Rob's arms. The large tail thrust the fish forward and then moved it back down into deeper water. Rob watched as it swam back out past the breakers, out past the reach of the moonlight.

September 19–September 26

Here Comes the Tide

BEACHES ARE IDEALLY SUITED FOR WEDDINGS; that's why so many of them take place there. That shimmering, changing, breathtaking backdrop. The ocean for your choir. Seagulls standing in for angels. A carpet finer than could be found in any of Solomon's palaces.

But few people actually live at the beach–or even near it. It takes planning and effort to get to paradise…

Janet felt a buzz in her pocket as she walked to her car and stopped to check her cell phone. It was a group text from her twin sister, Tonie.

"We're engaged!"

Above those two life-altering words was a photo of Tonie Grant in the Sarah P. Duke Memorial Gardens at Duke University, trying to look surprised as Alex Miller knelt in front of her. They were framed by a bower of wisteria that draped above them. Undoubtedly their friend Tom was crouched a respectful distance away to get the shot. You could practically smell those flowers.

Janet quickly texted back: "Happy for you!"

About an hour later, Janet's phone rang. It was Tonie.

"I can't feel my thumbs!" she laughed.

"Congratulations," said Janet. "Looks like you're going to get your tiara. You've only been trying them on since you were six."

Tonie laughed. She paused and said, "Can I ask you a favor? A big one?"

"Done," said Janet. "What?"

"Well, maid of honor—you will be, *won't* you? I need some help with Mom and Dad."

"You mean with Mom." Janet smirked. "And of course; I'd be honored to be honor. Now, what's up?"

"Mom has already started in on the *big-church-wedding thing*, but I don't want that."

"Yeah, well," said Janet. "You'd have better luck if *she* hadn't eloped. What do *you* want?"

"The beach!" said Tonie immediately. "I want us to be married at the beach. That's where so many of my happy memories are."

"Wow! Now *that* would be cool!" said Janet. She thought to herself for a moment and said to her sister, "Hmmm. Let me see what I can do."

"Twin power?" said Tonie.

"Twin power!" answered Janet.

With great energy and great effort, the course of even a mighty river can be changed. Mrs. Grant eventually—*eventually*—relented.

"What did she say?" asked Tonie, when Janet called her with the news.

"Oh," teased Janet. "That you were breaking her heart. That you'd regret this someday. That we'd have that church wedding when it was my turn. And just what should the colors be?" The two sisters cracked up over the phone.

That beach that Tonie desired for her chapel was Surfside Beach, South Carolina. Grants of different sorts had been going there since the 1970s. Such a pretty, family kind of place—just a couple of quiet miles of beach sandwiched in between noisy Myrtle Beach to the north and the towering hotels and condos of Garden City Beach to the south. Ideal.

The house the Grants always rented was part of a small complex called Portofino II, ten houses arranged in a square around one central swimming pool. As the guest list began to swell, it was decided early on that the actual ceremony would be for just immediate family and the couple's friends. Receptions would be held afterward in each of the respective families' states. Even so, that still meant about three dozen people would be coming. A group that large would need five of the ten units: one for the bride's family, one for the groom's, one for the guys, and one for the girls. And a fifth house, just for "staging"—everything from flowers to pedicures. Mr. Grant made the rental arrangements; Tonie and Janet took care of the who went where, parceling out the bedrooms and pull-out sofas.

Mrs. Grant set about to the task at hand. The Grants and the Millers were about to be fused. A new tribe. A new clan. Empires and industries have been created from this very act. Things must be done. Plans must be made. The marriage that follows is another thing altogether. Once the mooring on the dreamboat of wedded bliss has been tossed from the dock… well, good luck. But weddings are no accident.

Mr. Grant was involved in what was left of American manufacturing. Mr. Miller was his opposite number: a lawyer. Their wives now ascended to a status higher than wives: mothers of the bride and groom.

Each family had a surviving patriarch. The Grants' was Colonel Grant, though he had neither served in the military, nor was he southern. His ramrod-straight posture and sense of propriety made up for any lack of specific credentials. His wife—who had always been Maw-Maw to Tonie—was his mindful attendant. Across the aisle could have been Grandpa Miller, who was on the very last legs of a most colorful life—so colorful, in fact, that he was not invited. Many years earlier he'd left Alex's grandmother behind in his wake. Grandma would be coming, but with her second, more sensible, husband. And Alex's younger brother, Nick, would of course be there.

Alex and Tonie were both involved in campus theater, and from the ranks of the *dramatique*, their friends came. Both of them were adored by their circle and, well…the beach! Many signed on, and many more very much wanted to. Save the parents and grandparents, the crowd would skew young.

Two weeks out from wedding, Mrs. Grant was pleased. The big items on the bridal list—the dress, the caterers, the flowers—all had checkmarks by them. Everyone and everything were all in order to be marshaled to the beach. *That* dress was carefully placed into a white box and chauffeured to South Carolina as though it were the Shroud of Turin.

The big day grew closer, and the two sets of parents descended on the rental complex and set up camp. Now strategy was bid adieu; it was all logistics from here on in. Nick and Janet were tapped to play courtesy shuttle service: a nine-mile drive to Myrtle Beach airport. The two counterparts made an odd pairing. She was older; he was taller. There was an uncalculated but socially significant age gap between them. Janet did the driving. Once at the airport, Nick would alight to the curb and hurl the bags in the back. They made a good team. Janet couldn't help but notice Nick checking her out when he thought she wasn't looking.

Memorable was the late night they scooped up Alex's best friend, Tom. Apparently, his debit card had been fully functional for in-flight beverage purchases. When they got back to the complex, Nick had to pry him out of the rented Escalade. Tom had never seen the ocean in his whole life. After stumbling down the walkway stairs to the beach, he rushed whooping into the surf, billfold in one pocket, cell phone in the other.

Shanna arrived fresh from a breakup, becoming the temporary center of attention. Emily came with a marital prospect in tow. Steven and Sarah couldn't make it; they were in mid-run of something called "Backwards Shakespeare." And Barry turned up in a Hawaiian shirt so loud you needed earplugs.

Lastly, Janet and Nick picked up Maw-Maw and Colonel Grant, although a flat tire on the big Cadillac made them almost an hour late. Colonel Grant provided them with a complimentary lecture on punctuality for their trouble.

Everyone had now arrived.

On the eve of the big day, Alex and Tonie were in the clutches of their elders. They left behind enough restless, idle youth that a touch football game was organized down on the beach. Barry produced a football, still warm from Walmart. Guys versus girls it became, which was brilliant on the girls' part, as the guys miscalculated and held back, while the girls were ruthless. Tom intentionally missed an easy tag on Shanna, and she noticed. Janet did indeed trip Nick on purpose.

Two hours later, these same combatants and every other soul in the wedding were all sitting on long plank benches. It was the rehearsal dinner, courtesy of the Millers. The affair was touted as a Low Country–themed event. What was delivered—to a background of indistinct, taped instrumental music—was a man in a loud striped suit, who served up shrimp and grits and shaggy dog stories with a thick South Carolina accent. Mrs. Miller winced her way through it.

Saturday morning sailed in magnificently with the first pink peek of the sun.

At the staging house, there was someone to do makeup. Someone else did hair, and someone did nails, both manis and pedis. There was also a pressing and fitting station. The main floor of this particular house was filled with online-ordered flowers, bundle after bundle of them sitting in white five-gallon buckets half filled with water. Two kids who did carpentry for campus theater productions were busy building a bower in the carport. Janet saw little of Tonie but a lot of Nick; there was always one more errand to run, and they were both on call.

Everyone seemed to be having a good time—everyone except Janet. The happy chatter in the prep house was getting on her nerves, and she couldn't figure out why. Rather than spoil the mood, she took herself and her funk out for a walk and wound up sitting at the end of the boardwalk of the "Grant family house," staring off at the ocean. Nick was returning from a stroll on the beach, but when he spotted Janet, he made a beeline toward her as nonchalantly as he could.

"Hey, what's up?" he tossed out when he got to the foot of the stairs.

"Oh, I don't know," said Janet. "Just taking a break from the crazy."

Nick kicked his foot in the sand like he was Jimmy Stewart. "You want to be alone?" he asked shyly.

"Nah," said Janet. "I could use someone to talk to."

Nick smiled at the invitation. "I needed a break too," he said. "My mom has me running everywhere."

"Tell me about it," said Janet. "*My* mom just had a meltdown over the seating arrangements." She sighed and, looking over him back out to sea, said, "I don't know why I feel like such a spectator—such an outsider. I mean, she's my *twin sister*, for crying out loud."

"How would I know? I'm just the *little brother*, for crying out loud," he said, perfectly copying her inflection, and then he laughed. Janet laughed too.

"Nick? Nick? Nick?" came a voice from the top of the walkway. It was his mother. "We need you to make a quick run to the pharmacy," she said as she caught sight of him. "I've got a little list."

Nick smiled at Janet, and she smiled back. Off to the pharmacy he went, and Janet wished that she'd gone with him.

They were having trouble getting up with the pastor, who was already late. Maw-Maw didn't feel well. Platoons of chairs were being deployed in precision out on the sand to Mrs.

Grant's new specifications. Vases of beautiful flowers defined an aisle. A volleyball game was beseeched to relocate further down the beach and blessed when they did so. Four steady arms carefully lifted the now-completed and festooned arch up the boardwalk and down to the beach. Center stage, it was invested and fortified at the base with small sandbags. A table was brought and set in the foreground of the bower. Then on that table were placed two small glass vessels, each one filled with sand, and then between them, a larger, empty one.

The wind picked up throughout the day as the warm sand magnified the thermals. It was warm, but so what? It wasn't raining. In fact, the sky was blue and filled with enough fluffy white clouds to make a photographer weep. The wedding party was clustered at the bottom of the boardwalk stairs, and now each was released in turn. Finally, here came Tonie with Mr. Grant—Dad—arm steady and acting as her seeing-eye dog. He never once lifted his eyes from the uneven terrain while she just beamed.

There were four musicians, but they were there to entertain the wind. Occasionally, the violin broke through. The vows, when they came, were equally celestially dispatched, accompanied by the occasional "What? What?" from Colonel Grant, despite Janet's shushing. The two small vials were emptied into the large one, creating a commemorative dune that would, in the course of its life, end up in a closet somewhere. Mr. Grant surprised himself by crying; Mrs. Grant surprised herself by not.

And then it was over. Down came the flowered bower— rather unceremoniously, considering its recent state of honor. A bouquet was thrown from the top of the boardwalk stairs, and by unanimous prearrangement, Emily caught it, turning immediately to smile at her invited target. Pictures were taken of everyone everywhere: people leaping, mugging, kissing. Mrs. Grant swallowed hard when Tonie let Alex toss her in *that* dress into the surf. Hope they got that one.

With no possibility any longer of anything going wrong, it was on to the celebration of that fact—on to the party. A gorgeous sunset gave way to an equally gorgeous moon. That warm wind was now a welcome guest. Tiki torches appeared around the pool, and Janet went about with a lighter, Nick's hands sheltering the little flames. The caterers arrived in force. The resident plastic pool furniture was stacked on the other side of low hedges and just out of sight. Pretty tables and scrupulously counted glasses and silverware took their place. A main table at the shallow end of the pool faced a DJ setup on one side and a bar opposite it on the deep end.

People streamed into the pool enclosure and took their seats until a rough quorum was reached. Then out came the waiters, bearing prefilled champagne flutes on trays. Dad spoke. Mom spoke. Then the other dad spoke. Then the other mom spoke. And then Janet was handed a cordless microphone and cleared her throat loudly enough to qualify as a sound check.

"Okay," said Janet, with just a charming hint of slur. "Tonie is perfect; we can all agree on that. So think how hard it's been for me all these years." Janet looked squarely at Alex.

"Alex, when you showed up on my twin radar, red lights went off. Soon my sister is telling me about what she and Alex did that day. And the next day. And the next." Janet gave out a loud laugh. "Man, I kind of hated you there for a while. All I could see was that you were breaking up a great duo."

Maw-Maw was wriggling in her seat. Nick began to quietly giggle.

"But here's the thing," Janet continued, gulping her champagne in punctuation. She looked at her sister, sitting so close to her. "Alex, you make Tonie happy. Really happy. So, here's to you both, and to a new trio," she said, spilling the last of her champagne in the direction of the pool. She plopped back down into her chair, and all the grandparents started breathing again.

Mr. Grant was grateful for those last-minute dance lessons. He took Tonie's hand, and together they danced to a song that Tonie had selected, but no matter the particular music, it was the centuries-old dance of fathers and daughters. Now Mrs. Grant did cry.

The formalities out of the way, the younger folks could commit themselves and their still-pink livers to the consumption of more alcohol. Tom developed a particular move—a leaning backward with a circle swirl of his empty glass—that he used to summon the beleaguered wait staff. The one time he fell over, shattering his flute, Mr. Grant got up and spoke to him, but a new glass was provisionally provided. Save an occasionally glaring grandparent, everyone was happy and showing it—including a smiling Janet. The dancing became more outrageous; even the DJ, who had seen it all, was laughing. The Grants ordered up a ballad and danced that glad-it's-all-over dance, and the Millers joined them.

Alcohol and the specter of embarrassment lowered the contingent of actual dance partners. To both their surprises, Janet walked up to Nick and thumped him playfully on the back. "Come on; it takes two to start a conga line," she said and turned her back toward him. He clasped his hands at her waist, and she pulled him along the outskirts of the wedding party, the two of them cajoling, challenging, grasping at any protruding limbs. The DJ quickly picked a new song, and the conga line was in business.

The grandparents were long gone. Even the parents were yawning their last. The wait staff collected anything expensive and did a preliminary count as they placed objects into large gray tubs. Cones of plastic glasses appeared for those still thirsty and able. Now Tonie and Alex departed to cheers and catcalls, ascending the back stairs of the house that would be theirs alone tonight, courtesy of the Millers, who had apportioned themselves out to other domiciles.

Shanna made a pass at Tom. Tom was caught slightly unawares but was more than willing. It would be her bridesmaid dress that Maw-Maw found on top of the pool hedge the next morning.

Barry had thoughtfully purchased explosives the previous day, and a rowdy group headed for the beach with a large cardboard box and a fireplace lighter. Five or six artillery shells later, Tonie and Alex appeared on their second-floor balcony and supplied their royal waves to the group gathered on the beach. Their friends wouldn't find out until the next day that Tonie had been throwing up most of the time since she'd left them; a result of sun, champagne, nerves, and perhaps that shrimp from the night before.

Down on the beach, the bacchanalia continued. *Whoosh!* And then out over the ocean, *bam!* A brilliant phosphorous chrysanthemum appeared. Standing back at the very edge of the rocket's red glare, Nick and Janet gazed across the open sand at each other. Nick walked up to her and offered his arm.

"Need a friend?" he asked.

She smiled. "Yes." She pulled his arm around her waist and slipped hers around his. "And want one."

Janet turned them both away from the crowd and aimed them toward the pier, about a half mile down the beach. The bright moon hung in the sky above them like a paper lantern. They walked arm in arm in silence, the sand cool on their feet, the warm breeze coming in off the ocean, the sound of laughter disappearing over their shoulders.

As Seen from a Safe Place

EXTREME WEATHER DEFINES A REGION AS much as any factor. No one in Orlando worries about blizzards; no one in Omaha worries about hurricanes. Tornadoes, blizzards, and hurricanes demarcate the landscapes and the shared psyches of the peoples they afflict. A tornado is a sudden, terrifying knife thrust. The blizzard howls, bringing with it a smothering, helpless paralysis. And then there is the stalking gorilla that is a hurricane—and the dread, the waiting for that blow from its massive fist.

From his squat stool at the makeshift sorting table, Dan surveyed the garage. He saw box after box. There were columns of boxes, pillars of boxes. All of them spat up from the cellar, the by-product of a basement toilet that had overflowed and just kept on overflowing through that one weekend they'd left Omaha and gone out of town. His First Communion certificate was hiding in one of them; fifteen-year-old checks were hidden in another. A massive pile of artifacts and junk, the sacred and profane. Ruth's part of the mess was already done and in the dumpster. This was his, all his.

But being out here in the hot garage with this stuff was still better than being inside the house in the air-conditioning with Ruth. Of course, these piles in the garage and all the time he was spending out here, taking forever to deal with them… yes, this bugged her. But she was really still ticked at him for the big blowup he'd instigated with the kids on Labor Day. Whether it was Kristi, or Bobbie, or Dan Jr.—one of them had disagreed with him about something or other. But he didn't give an inch. No, not him. Dan and a 2015 Willamette Valley pinot noir unloaded on all three of them—especially Danny. This time, though, none of their three kids gave in either. And then, well, things got out of hand. Doors were slammed. Words were said. Ruth was already worrying that no one would come home for Thanksgiving. It sure didn't look like it from here. Sigh. He was resigned, but also content, to be out here in this humid purgatory.

A few hours later, Dan lumbered into the kitchen to get a drink. Ruth was glued to the little TV that she almost always left on. Over her shoulder he saw their local weatherman. The guy pulled back from a map of eastern Nebraska all the way out to the Atlantic coast. There in the bottom right corner of the little screen was a whirling red spiral with a 2 in the center of it.

"This hurricane is moving rapidly," the man on TV said.

Hurricane?

The weatherman continued. "Harry is expected to quickly grow in force as it…"

Harry. The red spiral had a name.

"...and veering away from Florida, Harry will now come ashore somewhere between Georgia and North Carolina." The guy finished, and a truck commercial came on.

"Dan, that hurricane could hit our beach house!" Ruth said with some alarm.

They'd been going as a family to Surfside Beach, South Carolina, for some twenty-five years. And to the same blue oceanfront house—Portofino II, 317C—almost all of that time. Their kids had practically grown up at that house. It was the scene of a thousand memories, a thousand family stories. Every year they counted down the days until they could all be there and together again for their week at the beach.

Dan shrugged his shoulders. "It's not our house."

Ruth gave him a sharp look. He grabbed a beer from the fridge and went back out.

He was back at his table. New drywall, new carpet, new this and that were one thing. But all these boxes, tubs, and crates—this was worse. Some of them were marked on the outside with faded dates that went back to before their move here twenty-two years ago. One more slow pan around the garage, and then he bent his head back down, the last scene from "Raiders of the Lost Ark" in his mind.

Truth to tell, though, Dan felt a little bit of that Indiana Jones vibe himself. Box after box of the unknown. It was not just the stuff he came across that he hoped he still had; it was the stuff he found that he'd forgotten he ever did have. He was rediscovering his own past. No wonder this was taking forever. He found his baseball glove from Little League; it was in near mint condition after seasons of accompanying him on the bench. Dan placed the orange-laced leather mitt tenderly into a clear plastic tub that held larger things, like his Lone Ranger rubber band gun.

He repackaged a bunch of old LPs from a damp-stained cardboard box into one of the clear storage tubs Ruth had bought. *Grand Funk Railroad. Quicksilver Messenger Service.* Hey! *Sgt. Peppers!* Next came a box of insurance and loan papers from the old house. But then he found this document: "Certifying that [name here] has witnessed Haley's comet at 41 degrees 20 minutes North Latitude—96 degrees 10 minutes West Longitude, March 22nd, 1986." It was 4:00 a.m. and a cold night. The famous comet had looked like a celestial Q-tip, but he was there.

It got late. When Dan came to bed, the TV was already on and tuned to the Weather Channel. That red swirl was now a three. And the cone of the hurricane had shifted north.

"Dan, it's a *three* now," Ruth said, her eyes still fixed on the screen. "It looks like it's headed for South Carolina. Aren't you worried?"

"Well, what can I do about that?" Dan answered.

He went to turn the set off, and she snapped at him. "Hey, I'm watching this!"

"Suit yourself," he said, tossing the remote on top of her covers and turning out his own light.

By the time Dan got up, Ruth was already down in the kitchen. Every TV in the house was on, and they were all tuned to the Weather Channel. She was parked back in front of the little TV, a blue coffee mug in her hands. She heard him. "Harry is a *four* now, Dan," Ruth said softly. "I texted the kids to see if they're following the storm. They all are. Kristi is very upset." She took a breath. "Myrtle Beach is still in the center of the cone. Surfside Beach, Dan. This is our special place, and it could…just…disappear."

There was an awkward pause. Dan turned away from her and told himself to just keep quiet. He poured some coffee and left the kitchen.

He was back at Watchung Hills Regional High School. The tassel from his graduation cap: "Class of '68." And his gold and white senior yearbook. Good thing that had been on a high shelf. Old friends—and old girlfriends—and all the nice things they'd written about him and his certain future.

A couple of hours later, in the late morning of a muggy September day in Nebraska, Dan dozed off at his table…

He was in some city—what city, he couldn't tell. He was supposed to meet his family somewhere, he knew that, but no matter in which direction he walked, he felt he was going further and further away from them, and everything grew more and more unfamiliar. He was lost. He saw that his pockets were bulging with stuff. They were heavy to the point of slowing him down. He shoved his hands into one pocket and then another and another, looking for his cell phone. He was frantically yanking out empty candy wrappers and money and old receipts. He pulled out a photo that he realized he must have taken. It was a picture of his whole family, without him.

Dan startled awake.

To shake off his drowsiness, he pushed the garage door button, and up the door went. *Let the neighbors have a peek at the Augean stables*, he thought. He walked to the mailbox. It was sunny and rather hot out; the sky was a searing bright blue. Not a single cloud. Everyone was either gone or hunkering in their air-conditioning. There was no "Harry" here.

Odd to think of the hurricane boiling up the ocean a thousand miles away. Up and down his street he looked. Everything so quiet, so peaceful, so calm.

Nothing in the mail but bills and catalogs. And a postcard. The front of it was a picture of two beach chairs set up at the ocean's edge, both vacant. "You could be here!" was boldly printed inside the red arrow pointing toward them. Dan flipped the card over and "You'll love our autumn rates" was blazed across the top, along with the name and 800 number of a Surfside Beach rental agency. He slipped the card inside the bills to keep it out of Ruth's sight. Dan shuffled up the driveway, put down the garage door, and went back to his post.

No sooner had he sat back down than the screen door opened from the kitchen. "The governor of South Carolina issued a mandatory evacuation last night," Ruth said. And the screen door banged shut.

Dan shook his head, but against his will, he found himself thinking of the little blue beach house. There was nothing between it and the ocean and the storm. He snapped himself out of it and moved on.

His next tub was a box of photos marked "1992." Ruth had already gone through her own pictures, mercilessly discarding blurry vacation and Christmas photos, and anything from Disney World that didn't have a kid or a character in it. Dan pried open the cardboard flaps. These were his, all right: double prints. He flipped open the first orange pouch, one of maybe fifty in this box alone. These were beach pictures. Surfside Beach, of course, taken on one of their earliest trips. In the very first photo that he touched, a beautiful young woman in a pale-blue two-piece bathing suit gazed up at him with a mischievous look in her eyes. *Wow! Ruth!*

He didn't hear Ruth walking up quietly behind him. She was coming out with another weather update, but looking over his shoulder she saw that girl in the blue two-piece suit. "Oh brother," she said instead.

Startled, Dan turned around, the deck of photos fanning open in his hand. Ruth took them from him and dealt them onto the fold-up table. Right off the bat, up came a shy little boy, who was maybe eight years old, tops. What a look of complete innocence. She dealt another snapshot. A girl of about eleven, hands on hips, glared straight at them. "Bobbie," she said, as though it were a compound sentence. "That child always did exactly what she wanted to." Two photos of a gorgeous sunset came up, the second with Ruth in the foreground. And next was a picture of a little girl finishing her seventh identical sand starfish; a blue plastic mold lay faceup next to it. "Kristi would have made two hundred of those starfish if we'd left her alone long enough." Ruth laughed.

She pulled out a photo, just of the kids. You could almost see them squirming, as they were obviously attempting to be posed. One girl had on an aqua-blue tankini with watermelons. A girl a little older than her had on a maroon tankini with dolphins on it. And the little boy was wearing trunks with Johnny Bravo on them. Dan took the photo back from her, and he studied it closely.

"Was this the trip where that big thunderstorm caught us on the beach?" he asked, with some emotion in his voice.

"Yeah," she said. She looked at him closely. *He does care,* she thought. "Yeah. I think you're right."

"Wow," said Dan, "that thing came out of nowhere."

"And we were way, way down the beach," said Ruth, "on the other side of the pier. It blew up fast. The sky got pitch black."

"We got sandblasted running back to the house in that wind. You couldn't even look straight ahead. And then it was like standing in the shower. We got drenched."

"Danny cried all the way back to the house," said Ruth.

"You know," he said, "we've been going to Surfside Beach longer than we've lived here." He looked up at her and sighed. "What a wonderful place." Dan smiled at her. Ruth pulled over a stool for herself and sat down.

Sitting together in the warm, close air of the garage, they began telling each other beach stories.

Like about that night the four of them spread a blanket on the dune in front of their house to watch the total lunar eclipse. Dan Jr. was in his crib upstairs, his baby monitor cranked up to eleven and still very much in range. His silly baby sounds crackled in the night air and made them all giggle.

Or about the skink that Kristi caught. It lived in a five-gallon bucket on the porch for a couple of days. Then Kristi wanted to watch TV with her new pet. The lizard got loose in the house during *Strawberry Shortcake*, and they never found it. Bobbie wouldn't sleep without the lights on.

They eventually got around to the time that they were caught in Hurricane Floyd's path and had to evacuate. That was in September of 1999, and their three kids were all in various stages of little. What should have been a three-hour drive turned into ten hours, crawling from Surfside Beach to

Columbia—and that didn't count the hour and a half it took them to get a tank of gas.

"Remember?" said Dan. "Highway 501 was like a parking lot. Brother, if you got out of those two lanes, good luck on ever getting back in again!"

"Which is why," continued Ruth, "we had to open the sliding doors on the minivan and hold Danny out so he could pee. Traffic was so slow that the girls and I had no trouble running out to the bushes and then back to the van. You didn't move a hundred feet in the time it took us to do it.

"You know, if you hadn't booked us that room at the hotel in Columbia before we left Surfside," Ruth said, "we *never* would have found a room when we got there." That gave Dan a little smile of pride.

"I remember Floyd hit Columbia about two a.m. and woke us all up," Dan said. "It was so loud! The kids were so scared. Every one of them was crying. We all huddled together on our king-sized bed in a big ball."

They each grew quiet, remembering that frightening time. Dan was suddenly back there on that bed. There was a storm raging outside, but it didn't matter. The only thing that mattered was that his family was together and they were all safe.

"Our poor beach," said Ruth, with just a couple of tears coming down her cheeks.

"It'll be okay," said Dan. "It has to be." He took her hand. "Come on, it's been hours; let's go see what's happening."

They stood together in front of the little kitchen TV.

A man was holding onto a stop sign with one hand and a microphone with the other. Water was dripping off of his bent elbows as he spoke, and trees were in a lashing frenzy in the background. Beneath him in block white letters was the single word *Live* in italics, and then in smaller font: Morehead City, NC. The guy was trying to shout over the wind. "Harry has taken a dramatic turn to the north. There'll be lots of flooding and plenty of limbs down in the Low Country, but it's going to be North Carolina's turn on this one."

Ruth and Dan looked at each other. The center of that red swirl was well above Myrtle Beach now. That meant that the brunt of the hurricane would be coming ashore far enough north that it would lessen any destruction down in Surfside Beach. On the radar screen over the map of the coast, there were lots of deep green bands sweeping well past their beach. Oh, people would be cutting jet ski–like donuts in golf carts in the flooded Portofino II parking lot. The beach would be a complete mess, but it would be cleaned up in a day or two. And one special blue house would still be intact. Maybe a dozen shingles ripped off, and maybe even some water would have snuck in under the roof and come in upstairs, like it did with Floyd. A ceiling stain had been there to greet them the next year they went. But the house would not only still be there, it would be just fine.

"Hey, Ruth. Maybe we could have it at the beach."

Ruth looked at him quizzically. "Have what?"

"Thanksgiving. Would you want to have Thanksgiving at the beach this year? Maybe we couldn't get Portofino II 317C at this late date, but maybe we could." Dan looked at her eagerly. "What do you think?"

Ruth was dumbfounded, but she broke into a large smile and nodded her head up and down.

Dan reached for his phone and pressed it awake.

"You calling somebody?" she asked.

"Yes," he said. Then: "Uh, no." His voice was quavering. "I'm texting Danny. I want to see if he'd come." Dan paused. "But first I want to text him that I'm sorry." He was asking her with his eyes if she thought it was a good idea.

"I'm such a jerk," he blurted out. He dropped his head and began crying.

Ruth raised his head with both of her hands until Dan was looking just at her. She kissed him. And kissed him.

October 17–October 24

For Want of a Shoe

HARRISON SHERWOOD RENTED PORTOFINO II-317C IN Surfside Beach, South Carolina, for this year's mandatory family vacation. Florida might have been nicer—maybe even Disney World for the kids—but that would have cost two or three times as much. Out of the question. You couldn't beat those October rates at a South Carolina beach. This was all expenses paid, and *he* was paying the expenses. You got to see the ocean; you didn't have to swim in it too. He always called the shots; they all knew what they were in for.

He and Margaret would arrive first, giving him enough time to contrive his usual set of rules and regulations; then the kids and their kids would begin reporting in. Another man might have taken pleasure in the fact that he had enough cash in his money market account to buy the place they were staying in and would maybe have relaxed a little, taken it easier. But Harrison had been raised on stories of watercress Wednesdays and banks that suddenly disappeared. His family's motto was "That's still good. You don't need a new one." That, and a well-earned distrust of the notion that things are sound, that you can be safe. Money was a matter of survival. Money was an outer wall of protection; spend it, and you grew weak.

Margaret truly loved the Great Man. She wasn't scared of his bluster. Unless he was at full steam, she could handle Harrison. Watching them from outside their relationship might make one wince. But it was not that way. They had their unconscious bargain that she would be responsible for smoothing over his brusque interactions with an irritatingly imperfect world. This job was not taken on out of weakness on Margaret's part, but gratitude. Long ago, when they had both been young, she had found herself in one of life's all-too-plentiful whirlpools—out of a job, responsible for a child who was the happy keepsake of an unhappy relationship. Life for her and her little girl went from grim to impossible. And as the water swirled around and around her in a dizzying depression, a hand was miraculously thrust toward her. It was Harrison's.

They pulled up to the beach house on their designated Saturday morning. It was a two-story structure, painted a cheery ocean blue and perched up on pilings that created a carport underneath. It was genuine oceanfront, as opposed to any of the many beach rental euphemisms, like "ocean view" or "ocean facing," phrases that essentially boiled down to "not oceanfront." In fact, in the ten-house complex that made up Portofino II, this was the northernmost oceanfront unit, and owing to the slight irregularity of coastlines, it curved out just a little from its neighbors, giving a wonderful view of the pier to the south or, turning up the coast, of Myrtle Beach.

They trudged their bags from the car up to the master bedroom on the second floor. Once invested, Harrison began an inventory of his temporary possessions.

"Where's the electric mixer? They said we'd have a mixer," he said, still looking at the printed list in his hands.

"Harrison, what do we need a mixer for anyway?" Margaret asked. She was just thrilled with the place.

"That's not the point," he said. "It says 'electric mixer' on the inventory sheet. Call up the rental office, and get me my mixer."

Of course. It was the easiest thing for her to do. Say yes and get the mixer, or else hear about it for the next week.

The kids didn't start arriving for a while. It was going to be just the two of them for now. It wasn't actually time off. Harrison never really took time off; "off" to him was "dead." So he made himself a wager. He would make enough profit trading stocks until the kids came in to pay for this whole vacation. Now *that* would make this all worthwhile. But come Monday, it also locked Harrison and Margaret into the New York Stock Exchange's timetable, effectively imprisoning them in the house from 9:30 a.m. to 4:00 p.m. Margaret just hovered about, asking him if he needed anything, granting herself the occasional sigh as she looked out at the ocean.

The thing about the beach is that not a lot of people go there for its internet access. So while the quotes are scrolling along the bottom of the CNN screen, and any market-shaking news occurs in real time, even the mightiest hunter is armed only with an internet service that constantly reminds you that you're supposed to be coated with sunscreen and sitting under an umbrella out on the sand.

Harrison had his eye on a couple of situations, both small-cap stocks. One in particular: Lone Star Bearings. Earnings were due to be released, and he knew vendors who said they couldn't keep these people supplied. They were in oil and gas repair, and the stock was very thinly traded. This latter fact made for delightfully illogical oscillations in the share price from time to time, swings that a trader with guts could jump on and ride like a Brahma bull.

Just near the close on Monday, on one large, indigestible block of shares, Lone Star Bearing was trading down five-and-a-half dollars, selling at that moment for twenty-seven bucks. Harrison leapt to his feet when he saw the symbol and its accompanying price lazily swim by on the bottom of the TV screen. He was yelling at the set, demanding, "Confirm! Confirm! Show me that again!" A few minutes later when the symbol again went by, the stock had picked back up fifty cents on only five hundred shares. Another minute, and it was up seventy-five more cents on another small trade. His five-and-a-half-dollar gift was now a four-dollar-and-twenty-five-cent gift.

It was 3:48 p.m.—twelve minutes left to trade. The laptop was sitting upstairs on the bed in the master, kitty-corner on an end table, in the spot with the best signal the place could muster. Harrison bolted. He ran around Margaret, jumping for the stairs. And at precisely 3:49 p.m., the irresistible force of Harrison's bare, right-side big toe met an immovable object: the plywood facing of the third step that led up the stairs to the waiting computer.

It would have still been close. It would have still been dicey as to whether he could have logged in on time, gotten a reliable connection, and made the trade. Had he made it, he would have been able to buy two thousand shares of good old Lone Star Bearing at twenty-eight and three quarters, and he could have sold it the next day when they did announce earnings at thirty-five and a half, netting himself a profit of $12,362 (pre-tax, of course). That's a lot of hush puppies and fried flounder. But when his toe rammed full force into that wooden cliff face, he might just as well have been Tasered.

He grabbed his foot and plunged backward onto the little throw rug in the entryway. When Margaret rushed to his side, his eventual first intelligible words above a mix of moaning and swearing were, "Is the market closed?"

They went out that night. It was a convoluted ploy on Harrison's part to fend her off from taking him to the emergency room. He thought that if he could make it through dining out, he could prove to Margaret that he was okay. That was his first blunder. Picking Seaside Smorgasbord was his second. Yes, it was cheap, but it also meant that his all-you-can-eat venture would be a painful round-trip hop every time he wanted something. After just one visit to the stainless-steel islands of gustatory enchantment, he stayed stubbornly put.

"Harrison, honey, are you okay?"

"I'm fine. Just fine."

"Can I get you some fried shrimp? You love fried shrimp!"

Of course he loved fried shrimp. He came here for the stupid fried shrimp. And if his toe hadn't kept continually interrupting him like a small child, he would have had a plateful of them in front of him right now. "No, thanks. I don't want fried shrimp tonight."

He limped into the passenger seat, and Margaret drove them home. They hopped together up the stairs, and he dropped gratefully onto the bed. She carefully peeled back his sock, ignoring his protests. His toe now looked like a small seedless watermelon, one that had either been left on the vine much too long or else had been lying in very wet soil. Margaret was uncharacteristically firm: Harrison was going to the emergency room first thing in the morning. Period. He tried to reason with her that tomorrow was the last day of trading before the kids got there, but his toe was on her side. It was late, they would sleep, and he could show her in the morning that there was no need for all this fuss.

But sleep was measured out in fitful rations that night, what with the unbearable pressure of a sheet and blanket on that toe. And in the morning, after a few tragicomic minutes of pretending that he didn't even have a big toe, he was slumped back onto the couch, cradling his throbbing barometer. It would be sandals—not shoes.

"Let's go, Harrison."

"Not yet. Not until the market opens."

"All right, but don't blame me if there's a crowd at the hospital." She meant that. He would have to sign off on that if he wanted her to let him watch TV.

"Okay, okay. But we've got to be back by lunch." Then that symbol—LSB—went by, up very sharply on heavy volume, at once both confirming and taunting his genius, and it took all the fight out of him.

Because of his self-imposed delay, they didn't actually pull up in front of Horry County General Hospital until just about 10:30 a.m. It was a very beige affair, with parking lot islands that had small palm trees on either end. Harrison winced his way to a bench while Margaret parked the car. She returned, and he hobbled in with her help through the automatic doors located under that ominous backlit sign—*Emergency*.

Not too bad, he thought to himself, surveying the large waiting room on his short hop to the front desk. *Just a few people. This shouldn't take long.*

They made their way to a large double window that faced into the room; one side was slid open. There were two nurses at the front, one young and one older. Both were stationed behind computer monitors, talking, and they continued talking as Harrison and his wife approached.

"Yes?" said the more severe of the two.

"I need to see somebody about my toe," said Harrison. "She thinks I broke it." He was pinning all the responsibility for this waste of time on Margaret.

It didn't dawn on him until it was much too late that his ardent claim that there was nothing at all wrong with his toe was completely out of sync with his demand for immediate attention. Eventually he realized that the nurse only actually heard remarks about his toe, only made notes about his toe, and completely ignored his insistence that he be seen right away. It was as if his hurt toe was all that she was interested in. Nothing is more frustrating to a man who demands attention than for that attention to be withheld. When the nurse was finished with him, Harrison was directed over to a grouping of industrially taupe couches, and he dropped down onto one of them in a stew.

Margaret wasn't sure what she was supposed to do in this situation. Harrison was giving her no lead to follow. He was frothing, but she felt that this large, clean, and orderly space was really quite soothing. She could have stayed there all day. Her obvious lack of agitation eventually got to him as the time dragged on. When he realized that she couldn't help him in this medical gulag, he finally chased her off, insisting that she leave and go shopping—do anything besides sit there and watch him be helpless like this. She didn't want to go, but she didn't want to draw his fire either. He'd call her on her cell phone when he knew something. Surely, this couldn't take more than an hour.

That hour went right by. A kid came in, crying loudly, his distraught father clamping a bloody cloth hard about his hand, trying not to cry himself. A few others passed through. An old woman arrived, brought in by the rescue squad. Emergencies that Harrison judged as trivial kept bumping his place in line, and he resented it. This was ridiculous. He was fed up. If only his toe didn't hurt so much. He called Margaret, yelling at her for the benefit of the nurses. After his little show, he was right back in front of the sliding window.

"Yes?" one of the nurses asked, not even looking up this time.

"It's been well over an hour!" Harrison fumed. "I have things to do!"

"I'm certain." Now she looked up. "Sir, we will call you when we're ready for you."

Back to his Naugahyde couch he sulked. The place was filling up, not emptying. A short, plump woman with unnaturally red hair came and plopped by Harrison, a seven-year-old boy in tow. The boy sat between them, his leg touching Harrison, who could see the boy's nose was producing two slightly green lava flows that ran down to his mouth. The boy sighed and absentmindedly licked the snot from his upper lip.

The redheaded woman was on her phone, oblivious to all else. The boy had a phone, too, but it hung listlessly at his side. Now he brought it up to face level and, sighing again, leaned himself against Harrison. Harrison's mind recoiled first; his body soon followed suit. No use. The more he leaned away, the more the boy leaned against him, until the kid was approaching horizontal. This was unbearable.

Harrison stood abruptly, and the boy's head cracked against the wooden armrest. He heard the kid let out a wail, but he didn't bother to turn around and see the red-haired woman look up from her phone.

He hopped up to the receiving nurse, just as he would have to a maître d'. He stood there while she talked on the phone, ignoring him, and mentally dictated a letter to the board of directors of this place. It calmed him down to think of communicating with those who he knew must be just like him. They would write him back, careful to thank him for his thoughtful complaints. The letter hung there, suspended in his imagination and awaiting his signature. And then it burst, just flashed away, exploded by a loud screech just out in front of the receiving doors.

Harrison turned to see a small silver Honda with blacked-out windows stopped half on the sidewalk. It was pulsing out a tremendous dull pound of music that pushed its way through the thick glass windows of the quiet waiting room. In the next instant, the car doors flung open, the sound racing out from inside it, enveloping two teenagers who bolted from the vehicle. A third came out from behind the driver's side, pushing the seat forward. Then he and one of the other kids were both pulling at a pair of legs, then grabbing the waist, then supporting the shoulders, of a fourth occupant. This kid's white tank top was soaked with blood.

The bloody boy's head hung very low, and the third kid in the group caught up the boy's legs. Together the four of them moved like one frightened crab across the remaining sidewalk and in through the airlock of the automatic doors.

"Help! Hey, somebody! Help!" The three boys were all shouting, their terrified words piling up on each other. They lurched right up next to Harrison at the receiving window. The sheer fear in their voices moved him out of their way.

He just stood there, looking down at the boy, watching the blood pool up on the fabric of the kid's shirt. His abdomen curved downward in the catch of his friends. Harrison stared at the little red sea filling up from two ragged holes invisible below. The boys shifted their friend in their arms, spilling some of that blood onto Harrison's exposed and throbbing toe. They weren't making any sense, yelling through tears, nothing of use. One of the nurses had pressed a button the moment the teenagers burst into the waiting room, and now two men in white came rushing through the double doors at the back of the place. They were up to the boy in an instant, tenderly laying him, curled now into a little ball, onto the gurney that they had brought with them. They raced him back through the double doors at the end of the room and disappeared, the sounds of his friends echoing as they followed after them.

And then it was quiet again. Completely quiet. An orderly with a mask on his face and gloves on his hands came out with a mop, a bucket, and disinfectant. Seeing Harrison's foot, he produced an alcohol wipe, and before Harrison had time to flinch, the toe was clean again. The two nurses were still at their posts. They sat back down, silently returning to what they had been doing just minutes before. The car outside on the sidewalk continued to pound away, alive with noise but uninhabited.

Harrison felt as though he were in an aquarium, as though he'd suddenly awoken underwater, everything about him thick and dreamlike. There was nothing in his mind now but the dull echo of what had just transpired. That itself didn't have a chance to last long. A black-and-white police cruiser with a palm tree on its door pulled up directly behind the silver Honda with its sirens screaming.

The high-pitched wailing out from the squad car overlay the deep rumble of the Honda. Two uniformed officers came running in, leaving both cars momentarily in duet, before a third cop turned the siren off. Now the three were standing right next to Harrison. Harrison, who was standing where a pool of blood had been a moment before. With his head still submerged, he could see the policemen and the nurses talking, but he couldn't hear them.

The cops were across the room and through the double doors and gone. Harrison stood there, numb. It was quiet for what seemed like a very long time, but time was not really time right now. Then, from behind those double doors, came a cry and a moan so high but so heavy, that it poured in through the waiting area like a thick fog. First, one voice, and then it was three. And then the voices faded off into low, soft moans, lower than the human heart can bear.

The cops came back through the double doors again, each with his arm on one of the boys. But the boys were spent now, limp; the officers supporting more than coercing them. The three boys were led out to the cruiser and carefully tucked into the back of the black and white, their heads crumpling to their knees when they sat down. Two officers got into the front seat, and the car pulled away. The third cop stayed behind on the sidewalk, speaking into his walkie-talkie as he leaned into the Honda and switched off the ignition. The pounding stopped.

Harrison had completely forgotten about his toe this whole time, caught up in someone else's bloody nightmare. But his toe brought him back into the waiting room. He looked now at his foot, regarding it as some unnecessary curiosity, as though it were irritatingly tapping on a window while he was trying to listen to something. Once again, there was that terrible and complete silence. Harrison couldn't think about sitting down again. He held onto the lip of the counter at the nurse's station.

From somewhere deep in his confusion he heard, "Mr. Sherwood? Mr. Sherwood?" The PA system was asking for him. In a few moments, a nurse with a clipboard was standing in front of him, saying his name like a question.

Now it was his turn to go through those double doors. Once through them, it smelled like a hospital, felt like a hospital. As they went down a corridor, they passed an old orderly slowly wheeling a bed; a still form lay under a red-splattered sheet. The body, the red-and-white shirt, the eyes, were all hidden now, but it was the kid. The man's gaze was focused only on the top of his rolling burden, and he passed silently by.

A nurse directed Harrison into a small curtained room off one side of the corridor, told him to sit, and left him. His head began to pound. His throat was dry. He was waiting once again, but his busy mind didn't notice the time. A few moments later a young man came in, bringing with him the clipboard from the clear-plastic pocket attached to the outside of the open door. He wore a fresh white coat, but there was a small red stain on the shirt underneath it.

Harrison couldn't hear the doctor talking to him. He just let the two of them, the doctor and his toe, talk. Something very strange was happening to him. He had begun to shrink; he was shrinking. Thinking of the dead teenager, and thinking of his own life, he was getting smaller and smaller and smaller.

The doctor finished, and Harrison looked at him a moment and then offered him a blank, "Thank you." The man said something about going for an x-ray, but Harrison didn't really catch it.

And then, as he was growing smaller still, he was left alone in the spare white room. He became filled with an urgent sense of foreboding. Smaller, smaller. The little room was now the size of an airplane hangar.

Harrison craned his head out of the doorway and looked down the long, tiled corridor. He looked, but he saw nothing. As he continued looking, he saw at the very end of the hallway the same old orderly who had taken away the dead boy. The man was pushing a wheelchair down the hall in Harrison's direction. Straight toward him, the old man came. Harrison's forehead began to perspire.

He jerked his head back into his room. The orderly showed up and wheeled in the chair, but didn't say a word. He lifted Harrison underneath the arm and guided him into the seat, clacked down the footrests, and carefully loaded Harrison's feet onto them. Then he pushed him out into the corridor, turned the wheelchair, and headed it back in the direction that he'd just come. He pushed Harrison down this long length of hall and turned the chair toward a dimly lit vestibule at its end. Harrison was having trouble breathing—trouble reminding himself to breathe. An elevator was waiting for them both, its doors wide open.

Into it they went. The man turned them around, facing toward the long, open corridor. The orderly pressed a button on a panel, and the brushed metal doors closed very slowly, shutting them inside, everything gone but their little cubicle. The elevator gave a small shudder.

The stainless-steel walls of the elevator began to pulse. Harrison and his life of numbers and his petty rules were dissolving. Layer after layer of him was disappearing, beyond his control. For Harrison, a horror built up that nothing, nothing at all of him would remain. Nothing. What had there been, anyway?

As the elevator began to lurch so slowly downward, he was convinced that by the time those doors finally opened, he would disappear entirely. His forehead was drenched. His shirt collar was soaked. His hair began dripping with sweat.

This slow descent was unbearable.

He was certain that his wasted life was ending. No time even for regret. The air was close now, getting harder to take in.

Soon he would be gone…completely…gone.

Finally, the elevator came to a shaking stop, but the old orderly did not move. Slowly, slowly, the doors began to part. Harrison clenched his eyes shut to shield them from he knew not what.

"Daddy?"

His eyes squeezed tighter yet.

"Daddy?" came the voice again.

Sharon? He cautiously opened his eyes. He saw Margaret and then his daughter Sharon. She was with her husband, Joel, who was holding hands with their daughters, Jessica and Jennifer. And little Steven was standing there too. They were all there in a big welcoming arc in front of the elevator. Harrison couldn't speak. His eyes went to every one of theirs, looking at each of them intently. The air rushed into his lungs in a cool, welcoming gulp. And then he smiled. He smiled, and he felt a warm tear washing over his wrinkled cheek. He looked up at the old orderly. He was smiling too.

They all waited around for him until he got his x-ray. Harrison was laughing. Margaret couldn't remember the last time she'd seen him laugh like this.

They waited until the doctor saw him again. Harrison was telling stupid, ancient jokes and making the grandkids giggle. He got a cast, and he made everybody sign it; the grandkids went first. As they wheeled him to the curb, they passed an earnest young boy shaking a can with an urgent-looking label wrapped around it. Harrison had them all stop. He searched around in his trousers until he came up with a twenty-dollar bill, folded it into fourths, and squeezed it through the narrow slot in the top of the can.

Today when Harrison walks along the beach, he must remain quite conscious of that toe of his. It hangs just that much lower than all the others. And if he does not stay aware of it—if he is distracted by thoughts of work or money, or the cares of this life—if he does not stay with the crimson setting sun, with the kaleidoscope of gulls, or with the clouds hung like red sheets fluttering over the ocean—then that toe will catch him up, get itself caught in the sand, and bother him for days.

October 31–November 14

By the Light of the Silvery Moon

ALICE HAD REALLY GOTTEN TO LIKE driving. Or more precisely, had gotten to like driving again. All these years it had always been Walter who'd driven them anywhere and everywhere. Now that Walter couldn't drive anymore, it was her
turn again. He was back at the beach house, taking a nap. The
chemotherapy he'd had back home had just exhausted him,
and with the lingering nausea, it was just as well he was asleep.
Honestly, Alice couldn't remember the last time she had driv-
en alongside the ocean, just by herself. It would have to have
been all those years ago, back when they were newlyweds and
she still had that little red Dodge of hers, "Penny." It was the
car they both had known had the best chance of making it to
Surfside Beach and back. Walter had driven them out in it, but
then he'd let her do most of the driving once they'd gotten to
the beach. He just never got the hang of that car.

Now she drove a minivan, something comfortable for him
to ride in. This time it took them two days to get down from
Pennsylvania, since she'd been the only driver. It wasn't just
him being tired; it was also his stiffness. They would get out of
the van and move around every couple of hours, just like when

the kids were little. "That's no way to make time," he would have said once. No matter this time; they weren't in any hurry. Fools rush.

It was Walter's choice to come back to the beach one last time; his decision, really. But Alice was certainly happy about it. "Our favorite front yard," they'd always said about the place, the same place they'd rented all those years. And those winter rates! You got a month for the price of two or three days in July. After the kids were grown and gone, and they were no longer tied to the public-school calendar, they never again rented right in the middle of summer. They always booked two weeks and returned at this time of year; it was their secret season.

It was kind of funny to be coming back to the beach this way. Same time as always, but now it would be his last time. The doctors were pretty firm about that; it was more like being talked to by your parents than by your peers. Alice and Walter had already been dealing with this for a while when the email from the realty company came reminding them that "their" weeks would be up for renewal. "Why not?" he said when he saw it. "I'd hate to lose our time slot. We might not get it back!" And he laughed. No, this trip was not to be a funeral procession. Nor was it to be a wake. Just their time, that was all—just like the rental company said.

Walter's attitude took all the pressure off. There were some logistics to work out, even some medical records that had to be sent down, just in case, but it was clearly going to be a vacation, leaving the work of worry and the work of sorrow back home behind them.

So there was Alice, for the umpteenth time at the Piggly Wiggly, all by herself. Of course, that's how it had always been anyway. There hadn't been kids to buy for in a long time; even so, the last several years she'd gone and picked up the basics. This time there wouldn't be those long restaurant nights out. It didn't matter. She liked to cook. She liked to keep a nice house. Yes, she knew she was traditional, but after the war, traditional seemed like a nice thing to want to be.

Walter was insistent on staying active. Yes, he took a lot of naps. Sometimes he took several in the course of the day. But he fought the idea that he was now somehow out of the game, just because he was sick—okay, just because he was dying. Wasn't his mind just as sharp as ever? If they didn't want him to drive, fine; don't fight that battle.

She loved the sunrises; he loved the sunsets. He wanted every day at sunset—if he possibly could—to be walking on the beach with Alice. He even set the alarm on his wristwatch for half an hour before, to make sure that he didn't miss it. He changed that alarm every day to adjust for the sunset change. It was only a matter of a couple of minutes or so, but he enjoyed the mental exercise. And on his good days, they would walk all the way to the pier.

Appetite or not, he made a point of going out to lunch. Plenty of places nearby had a view of the ocean. He would order food, even if he barely touched it, just so that his plate could keep hers company. They had always been like that with each other. Close, very close. They were grateful souls, these two. You could chalk that up to the war too.

His illness brought them nearer to each other still. Of course, it couldn't be the kind of closeness newlyweds have—yet it was like that. They were more playful with each other than they had been in years.

He noticed, then, while picking at his salad at the Lazy Seagull Café, that Alice was not so much looking at the ocean as she was looking far, far beyond it.

"Yes?" was all he said, taking her hand first.

She didn't answer but smiled when he touched her. It wouldn't do to say, "Oh, nothing." He could sense that she was already missing him. They'd talked about it out loud one time; no need to do it again.

"You see how the waves just keep coming and coming?" Walter began, without any reference. "They just keep coming, without any end, never stopping. They don't stop, Alice." He sighed. "It's not so much the waves themselves, you see; it's the power that sends them to us. That's the part that's eternal, that power. It doesn't make a difference how it's expressed in any particular wave; it's never going to stop. Those waves are us, darling." He pushed back his thin, white hair with his hand. "A long, long time from now, your wave will come ashore, just as mine is coming ashore now, and we'll meet all over again. And while waiting, I shall be very, very patient." He chuckled. "That will be something new for me."

She heard his words. She didn't really reflect on them much, because she knew what he was trying to do. Sitting there almost beside him, looking in exactly the same direction together, a tear came up and drifted down her cheek. When it let go of her, it landed on his hand. And when it did, he squeezed hers and wouldn't let go.

Ben and Eloise came by on their way to Florida. They lived back in Philadelphia now. It was nice to have company. At the end of the day, Ben and Walter ended up on the upstairs open porch, while "the girls" were off doing something or other. Each man had a freshly mixed stinger in his hand, although Ben's drink was the more generous.

"Hey," said Ben, "I saw that plaque the university put on the Anderson Building. Congratulations!" He saluted Walter with his drink.

Walter hoisted his stinger back. "Here's hoping the bronze part of me holds up better."

They watched together as a flock of about nine or ten pelicans flew their V just above the ocean, crossing the sky in CinemaScope, until finally they were silhouetted against the mountainous, scarlet clouds hovering out above the Atlantic.

Ben put his hand on his old friend's knee. "Walt, anything you need?" he asked, making sure he had the man's gaze.

"Thanks, Ben," Walter replied. "No. We've had a little time to get things set up. All pretty squared away." He smiled at Ben and touched his knee in response. "Thanks, pal."

"Anything you *want*?" asked Ben earnestly.

Walter leaned back and laughed. "Oh, that one's too easy." He paused, sending all the warmth in his look that he could to his friend. "Just one extra day."

After their company left, Alice cooked up a surprise little outing to Brookgreen Gardens. They'd gone there a lot before the kids had come along. Such a pretty place. The morning was cool, with a pale-blue sky. She was cleaning up the breakfast dishes when she told Walter of her plan. A picnic lunch was ready—the works!

"What day is it?" Walter asked.

"Why, silly, it's Tuesday."

"I knew it," he said, with a forced little laugh. "A weak day. No wonder I feel weak as a kitten." His eyes were saying, *Sorry*.

Alice dropped the little dish towel in the sink and went over to him and knelt at his side. There was no alarm in her movements. It was more a sense of just wanting to know how he really felt.

"Well, you're in luck," she said, after a moment. "Today happens to be a strong day for me. In fact, Tuesdays are my strongest day of the week!" She laughed at him and asked playfully, "Want to go to Brookgreen Gardens, sailor?"

He laughed back with her. "If you're buying!"

There wasn't even that much trouble getting him down and in the car. Alice drove. It was only ten miles, but they just hadn't gone in years. It really was lovely. Acre after acre of beautiful grounds, and those massive, intimidating art deco bronzes. Alice made a game of driving around the grounds and positioning the car in such a way that the best view was on the passenger side. Down would hum the electric window, and they'd look for a while, and then move on.

There was the *Saint James Triad*, the voluptuous bronze nudes each resting in and out of a flat, square, bronze frame, the sensual contrasting with the geometric. And here were the famous *Fighting Stallions*. Thirty-odd years ago, just to get a punch on the arm from her, Walter called it the "Dueling Dicks."

They stopped in front of *Eternal Youth*. It was just like the one put up in the American Cemetery near Saint-Laurent-sur-Mer. An ageless, bronze youth, with arms outstretched—a remembrance of the dead at D-Day.

Walter studied it intensely. Alice leaned quietly back and studied him. She noticed the way his white hair wisped its way down that old, wrinkled neck. Almost unconsciously, her hand drifted up his back to pet it. She pressed her fingers into the thin snow at his nape. He sighed.

Surprisingly, Walter began to feel stronger over the next few days. They were happy about that, as Greg and his wife would be coming with the grandkids the following weekend. Walter insisted on taking longer and longer constitutionals, and Alice took to calling him "Old Show-Off." He would walk backward, saying, "Look at me! Look at me! I'm robust!"

The next days were quiet, long, and tranquil. Every sunrise different. Every little walk turning up something interesting. There were calls from the kids and calls from friends, but they had their own peaceful little world.

They were on one of their sundown beach patrols when Alice thought she saw a shark—a big one—being pushed by the surf headfirst toward the beach. It didn't really seem to be swimming; it looked like it was being washed in, helpless.

Walter hesitated, but Alice ran right to the shoreline. The big dorsal fin rolled itself drunkenly over in the surf, gray on one side, white on the other. Only it wasn't a fin, it was a wing; the wing of a stingray. It flapped the surface of the water in a slow roll. This stopped even Alice in her tracks, and she slowed to a walk, moving quietly closer to it as Walter caught up to her.

What would have been a big shark was still a good-sized ray, probably four feet across the wings. The body itself was quite stout and blunt, like a gray football. Then there was that long tail, like a coachman's whip.

Standing at the waterline, Walter and Alice could see that the creature wasn't making any progress at all against the surf; so close now that it sailed in and out with every wave, retreating with the tide too. It flapped its wings, but in no particular rhythm and with no strength. The tide was still going out, and that left the stingray farther and farther up the beach with every retreating surge. At last, inevitably, one large swell rolled the animal over and over, its wings flapping across its body like a loose overcoat. When this wave pulled back, the ray was up on the beach and on its back, white belly and white wings up, the small mouth at the front of the football, gasping.

Alice and Walter looked at each other and then looked up and down the beach, hoping to see someone who might know about these things, who might be able to help. There was not a soul to be seen.

Alice walked cautiously up to the creature. The ocean now barely reached the animal's wings. The ray was clearly beached, and would be for hours until the tide returned.

Alice looked at Walter, who was taking this all in. "Walt, he's dying."

Walter heard her. He knew from looking at the heaving body of the thing that she was right.

"He's stranded, Walt, and he's exhausted. He can't last much longer up here on the sand."

Walter knew what she was starting to think. He knew there was no way that Alice would abandon the animal.

"You think it's really in danger?" he asked. He didn't think it wasn't, but his question cut through a lot of discussion.

"Definitely," said Alice, with a firm nod.

"What about the tail, the stinger thing?" he asked, almost helplessly.

"We'll just have to be careful. We'll just have to see. I think he's too tired to really use it."

Before they could do anything, they had to flip the animal over. They each grabbed one wing together, backing up and crossing over the body of the creature. Walter couldn't help but think of all the times he'd been flipped over in the hospital. This part wasn't all that hard; the football body high-centered the creature, and he rolled over, the wing coming out of their hands and suddenly slapping the sand.

They moved to each lift up the flap of a wing, but they weren't looking at the whole animal; they were just staring at its tail. The wing that Walter held pulled out of his hands, and they both jumped back, startled. They tried it again. The tail showed how spent the ray was; it moved like a listless garter snake. They tugged at its wings, both of them walking backward toward the sea. The stingray was heavy and seemed heavier still because of the friction of its body against the sand. It was work, and Alice had to balance her efforts out with Walter, who was not able to pull as strongly. They caught a break when a bigger wave sent a thin sheen of water past their feet. They were able to use this bit of water to hydroplane the ray on its belly, gliding it out into the shallow water.

The water was cool—almost cold—but bearable. They didn't know what to do next. Walter was quite obviously ready to let go immediately. He held on only because he wouldn't leave Alice with the ray all by herself. Now the animal was wriggling its wings, the tips curling like an enormous tongue.

Once they got it to where the water was rushing past their knees, Walter asked, "Now what?"

"Believe it or not, this is the first time I've ever done this!" Alice shouted. They both laughed. They were so happy at having saved the animal's life.

The two of them were staring at that whip, which was now moving more animatedly. "I think we let go on the count of three, and then both run like crazy," Walter said, still laughing.

Alice did the honors. "One! Two! Three!"

They flung their arms up in unison and yanked their feet out of the ocean, turning back to the shore. As they got a couple of strides away, Walter lifted his legs up and down in an exaggerated style, like a slow-motion drum major, which caused Alice to double up with laughter and grab her knees. Once completely clear of the water, they both flopped down on the sand, hugging and laughing.

They looked up finally, wondering if they might still be able to see the stingray.

"Look!" Alice said, pointing.

The animal hadn't gotten very far at all from where they'd released it. It helplessly beat first one wing and then the other, smacking the surface of the sea, but again, the ocean was driving it back to shore.

They yelled, "Come on! Come on!" It was no use. They watched the whole prior scene repeat itself. In a matter of minutes, there was the ray again, lying on its back, stranded on the beach; in fact, it was only a few feet farther down from them than it had been the first time.

Walter and Alice looked at each other, puzzled, feeling helpless themselves. Still, there was no one else in sight.

"He's exhausted," said Alice.

Walter nodded back. "He doesn't have a chance unless he can get some strength back. We can get him back out there," he said with conviction.

"We'll have to," said Alice. "And hold on to him. We have to let the ocean run through him, run through his gills, until he's strong enough to fight the current. It's like he can't catch his breath."

"But the stinger..." Walter said, trailing off.

"I know," said Alice. "We'll just have to take that chance." She paused. "Hey, remember Androcles and the lion?"

"You're right," Walter said. "It could be worse. It could be a lion." They laughed.

"Shall we?" said Walter, sweeping his arm in the direction of the stingray.

And they repeated their end of the process, again rolling the animal over, again dragging it as best they could manage, tugging its weight against the sand until they got the help they needed from the ocean itself, the same ocean that had pushed the creature back to them.

They took him out to sea farther this time, well past the break of the surf. They were not as afraid as they had been the first time, even though now they were out in water up above their thighs. There would be no speedy exit. This was his territory, not theirs.

They stayed out there for what seemed like quite a while. It was peaceful past the surf break, like they were in their own little pool. Their charge was rather docile, not giving much indication of whether it was getting better or worse. For just a moment, Alice had the image pass through her thoughts of herself and Walter, each holding one of their children's hands as the child had learned to walk.

Walter noticed first that the undulations, the ripples of the wing he was holding, were becoming more rhythmic, more muscular.

"Hey, he's coming around!"

It was obvious to Alice too. The ray was trying to pull forward.

"How do you jump off the back of a tiger?" Walter said, grinning. "Is this the part where we remind him that we saved his life?"

Before Alice could make any reply, the stingray suddenly moved. With a strong, forceful push of both wings, the creature pulled itself out of their grasp and moved into deeper water, descending as it went forward. In a moment, it disappeared out of sight completely.

"Alice!" Walter shouted, almost as a reflex. They froze, not knowing if it was safe to move, scanning the water on all sides. Then they both began to retreat slowly backward, staring at the water in front of them. They had absolutely no idea what might happen next.

"Walt!" Alice yelled, pointing her finger about fifteen feet ahead of them.

The ray had risen to the surface again, again slapping the water with its wings.

"Come on! Come on!" Alice said, her jaw set hard.

"Come on! Come on!" Walter took up the cheer.

This time the animal was making progress. His wings dipped back into the ocean, carrying him down under the sea. Walter and Alice kept backing themselves out toward the shore, watching the water but unafraid. One more time, and then again, the stingray came to the surface and then dove below. By the time their feet were back on firm sand, the animal was well over a hundred feet out. They both watched as just one part of a wing broke through the surface for a last time, then disappeared. And that was that. *Sorry, Death. Not today.*

They collapsed onto the sand, but they weren't laughing this time. They sat, peering out over the surface of the water, tired and content.

That night was sweet—sweet indeed. Alice made a big bowl of pasta. A bottle of red wine was produced. And they told the story of the stingray to each other again and again. What they thought. How scared they were. Loud, laughing. They were kids again.

When the wine was gone, and while Alice was cleaning up the little bit of kitchen mess, Walter made his apologies with a kiss on the cheek, a sideways hug, and an "I love you," and headed upstairs to bed.

It was still dark out when Walter opened his eyes. He rolled to his left. The clock by the bed read "6:54" in big red numbers. *Yes!* he thought. Every day Alice got up to see the sunrise. Walter didn't mind, and he couldn't bear to miss a single one with her. But it was always Alice—good old, reliable Alice— who managed to get them up and out there, shivering on that upstairs deck, blankets wrapped around them, to see a new day pop out. And then she would tuck him back in—a most lovely, welcome little ritual—with her kiss on his head, and whisper, "Off to Dreamland." Finally, it was *his* chance!

"Hey," he whispered. "Hey, sleepyhead, my turn for a change. Say hello to a brand-new day."

Alice was so quiet. Not even a shrug. Walt reached out his arm and brushed her cheek with the knuckles of his left hand. And then that hand shot back to him. Cold. So cold. He didn't move. He didn't breathe. Now he called out, "Alice?" And then "Alice?" Finally, "Alice!"

He just lay there beside her for a while. His fingertips went out to touch her cheek, to stroke it. He could only think of touching her.

"Alice. Oh, Alice," he said aloud. "Now what?" And then he propped himself up on his elbow, hovering above her to kiss that dear, dear cheek.

Walter lay back on his pillow, as heavy, as exhausted, as sick at heart as he'd ever been. His breathing passed from rapid and panicked, to almost negligible.

The dark ceiling that hovered over him began to go from black, black, to gray. His tired head turned to the left to see the bottom of the sliding door drapes begin to brighten.

He pushed himself up. Walter looked at her still figure.

He made himself get out of bed, with Alice in his every thought. He shuffled, he staggered, to the sliding glass door. He pulled the curtain across from in front of him. Walter leaned against the door handle and opened it with his full weight. One more glance at the bed, to make certain she was there.

Now he went through the door and out onto the deck. If he was shivering, he didn't notice. The sun began to crown,

the first bright rays shooting out toward him across the open water. The waves. The golden waves, each crest shimmering in the new sun. The waves, coming in and coming in. How they came in!

O Little Town of Surfside Beach

ONCE AGAIN, IT WAS MELANIE'S TURN to host Christmas. After the fiasco that had taken place at her house three years ago, she knew that she had to do something…*new*. She thought, *What if we all went away somewhere this time?* And that one little thought—innocent, seditious—became a snowball rolling down a holiday hill, capturing members as it picked up steam, until all three related families protruded from it. Once the idea was universally accepted, the sisters-in-law—Melanie, Carol, and Denise—took charge of the proceedings and began to make it real.

CHRISTMAS VACATION was in block print on the whiteboard over the phone in Melanie's kitchen. Okay, go away, yes…but *where?* Potential destinations were auditioned on the board and then scrubbed off. "How about the mountains?" ventured Denise. That got few votes. "We live in Minnesota. Why would we want to pay to see snow?" Carol offered, "Honolulu," and that would have been everybody's choice…if they could have driven there…and back…in a week.

No, it had to be on the East Coast, had to be within reasonable minivan range. And it had to be warm too—or least

as warm as they could all afford. The ocean was soon a unanimous vote. North of Virginia Beach was erased as too cold. South of Hilton Head was wiped off because it was beyond the agreed-upon length of string stuck into central Minnesota. In the end, an area unabashedly called the Grand Strand, ended up remaining amid all the smudges on Melanie's message board.

The beach! This could be Melanie's redemption. The raw turkey, the closed fireplace flue that drove everybody into the snow-packed backyard until after the fire department left—it would all be forgotten. *The beach*. It made Melanie tear up just to think about it.

The chosen destination was Surfside Beach, South Carolina. "The Family Beach." That had to be a head start for a merry Christmas. The internet made it all look so beautiful—and cheap, really. Their search criteria narrowed them down to Portofino II–317C. Four bedrooms, three full baths, and a living room with a sleeper sofa; that should divide roughly into twelve people. They each took the "360-degree virtual tour," and then Melanie, Denise, and Carol got together in Carol's kitchen to parse out the real estate, tribe by tribe.

"How about putting Mom and Dad in that little bedroom on the first floor?" Melanie suggested. "It's tiny but right next to a bathroom, which is all that Dad will care about."

Carol volunteered herself, Tom, and little Jennifer for the back bedroom on the second floor, the one without an ocean view. Earl and Melanie were awarded one of the master bedrooms facing the ocean, while Denise and Jim took the other. The group's three teenagers would be corralled on the pullout sofas in the living room. There, all done. Presettled in

cyberspace so there would be no fighting when they actually got there.

Like the Israelites leaving Egypt for what they thought might be a week on the sand, the three families each gathered up their most precious Christmas ornaments, the treasured relics of countless holidays past. The faded green-glass globe that came over from Germany with Grandma—or was it Grandpa? The little carousel horse missing the left rear hoof that Carol herself had teethed on and swallowed. And the ornaments that Melanie's two kids had gotten that year they'd been in the big downtown production of *Peter Pan*; the prop manager had made them out of swatches of their costumes. They packed all these as tenderly as Joseph's bones and tucked them in the sport trailer hitched to Melanie's van—and the Ark of Christmas was on the move.

Off their little caravan set, across a great breadth of America. The men in the group determined that they had enough adult drive power to make it straight through from Saint Cloud, which would save them the cost of a motel. But Melanie insisted this wasn't going to be a cheap Christmas. Besides, she said, if they weren't going to Hawaii, the least they could do was go to a Hampton Inn. She used that "besides" argument a lot, especially when anything involving money came up. The three husbands knew the sisters-in-law were going to end up calling the shots on this one, and they plotted out the driving shifts accordingly.

They were a bright-spirited bunch of winter refugees. A reverse migration: people going from Minnesota back to the sea. Sometime around midnight, while climbing up the mountains of North Carolina toward Asheville, they found that

Hampton Inn, after all. Time for a night's sleep. Better to take on the mountains in the daylight.

The next day began as a beautiful, crisp, Appalachian morning. Most of the group was partaking of the continental breakfast, and everyone was complimenting Melanie on her decision to make them spend the night when Jim came yelling into the lobby. The Styrofoam plates were abandoned as they all rushed out into the parking lot and followed him all the way back to Melanie's van. At first glance, nothing seemed out of the ordinary. But wait—where was the sport trailer?

Gone.

All those ornaments. All those memories.

Gone.

All that remained was just a handful of half links of chain scattered on the pavement. They hadn't even stopped for nine hours, and now over fifty years of Christmas history was gone.

They gathered around the back of the van, where Melanie bent down and picked up some of the half-moons, trying to comprehend what had happened. She looked around at the stunned faces of the others, her eyes filling with tears. A silent, impromptu wake of sorts was held. No one could really bring themselves to say much of anything. It was too large a blow to the holiday psyche to be readily absorbed. All of their ancient Christmas treasures—a list too long to comprehend—all of it out there somewhere, in the hands of wicked strangers. That kind of grief can only come out with nightfall and alcohol, not sunshine and coffee.

Melanie just couldn't take it. She cried all the way to the rest stop in Columbia. When they stopped to refuel, she burst out of the van, swollen-faced, her eyes still streaming, begging everyone's forgiveness. It was pitiful. There is power in tears and abject prostration, and forgiveness was quick in coming. Tom said something reminiscent of a Hallmark card, like, "Christmas is more than ornaments," which produced an assenting murmur in the group. By the time they reached "the Family Beach," the additional long hours of asphalt-and-white-line meditation had given it time to sink in, allowing the loss to be dealt with somewhat.

Besides, the excitement of their arrival promised the whole venture a fresh start.

The men were duly impressed with the property. The closed swimming pool was of no use to them whatsoever, but it added to the place's cachet nonetheless. They were equally taken with the private walkway to the beach. All that lumber, and the engineering and architecture that came with it, to get from the back end of the house out to the shore. The women were inclined to focus on just how small the total living area actually was now that it was no longer filling up a computer screen. But thanks to that meeting in Carol's kitchen, they had it all worked out among themselves before the men returned from their first trip to the Super Walmart they'd passed coming into town.

While the kids slow-walked with Grandpa and Grandma to the pier, Melanie, Denise, and Carol sat at the dining room table adjacent to the kitchen and convened the College of the Cardinals—the culinary edition. This was about *the* dinner— Christmas dinner—which had taken on a much more emotional tone, what with the unthinkable loss of all their family treasures. A dozen or more "we always" traditions needed to be reconciled into a single Christmas feast, now that there was only one kitchen. Okay, sweet potatoes. Tipsy sweets? Melanie didn't drink, but Carol sure did, and she shot her a look when Melanie started to offer another recipe. After the tragedy of the trailer, Melanie felt too guilty to object. There would be tipsy sweets. One by one, each of the courses passed by for review. At last, the white plume of Carol's cigarette ascended off the back porch, signaling that the Christmas menu had been settled.

The trio now decamped to the Piggly Wiggly. This grocery store was more unfamiliar to these women than the ocean. Much of their specific menu was waiting for them back in the aisles of Minnesota. After all, South Carolina is not Minnesota or New Jersey or Texas; it's flapjacks or pancakes or griddlecakes. Is it soda or is it pop? Or is it soda pop? A shopping cart in Minnesota becomes a buggy when it's in South Carolina. A rose may be a rose may be a rose, but a supermarket is not a supermarket is not a supermarket. Still, like the funny local commercials on TV, the boiled peanuts, the moon pies—all the oddities repeatedly offered aisle after aisle were taken as confirmation of adventure.

A Christmas tree was another matter. Feelings were still raw about the absence of what had hung on so many trees before; however the business of the tree itself would still have to be addressed. But no one could agree on what *type* of tree. Fake ones were too expensive, and there would be no spot for one going home; not to mention the whole issue of who got to keep it. The live tree that the men lobbied for would have forced the teenagers to sleep upright, and would have cost the equivalent of a night out at a fancy tourist restaurant. Miraculously, little Jennifer came up with an unbeatable idea, an idea so cheap and precious that everyone bought into it: a paper Christmas tree. Eight feet of butcher paper, two boxes of crayons, and it kept everyone busy that whole day it rained.

The next day it rained off and on again, except this time they didn't have any cute art projects for people to do. But *It's a Wonderful Life* was on TV in rotation, the women were busy with preparations, and everybody generally kept out of trouble.

When it was foggy and rainy the day after that, and *It's a Wonderful Life* again relentlessly played on and on in the background—well, something was on the verge of snapping in Melanie. Maybe it was the rain. Maybe it was the gnawing guilt she still had about the lost trailer. Maybe it was having to say "excuse me" so many times she felt like screaming, expected as they all were to work just as much as if at home—except in about 40 percent of the space. In her disgruntled condition, Melanie took note with envy at how much chardonnay Carol required to sustain her cheeriness.

This whole trip had been Melanie's idea, and she could feel Christmas slipping through her fingers. She was desperate to get her turn at getting the holiday back on track. She caught a splashy ad on TV for the "Christmas Extravaganza"—some type of holiday spectacle at a big arena up in Myrtle Beach—and she latched on to it as her way to reboot that goodwill-to-all-men spirit.

Tickets for the show were expensive, and Melanie's hopes were correspondingly high. It was, after all, a dinner show; that sounded classy and promising. However, on arrival at the venue, they learned that "classy," in this case, translated to half of a very small chicken, that "Christmas soup" was cream-of-potato soup in a plastic mug, and that a majority of the plate was taken up by one very large biscuit. Moist towelettes were provided in lieu of silverware; apparently Santa ate with his fingers at the North Pole. They sat through a large musical number with a whole squadron of southern belles parading the length of the arena in their Christmas-tree hoop skirts emblazoned with flashing, colored lights. Then came the Elvis impersonator. Late Elvis. He sang "Blue Christmas," and conveyed a sort of holiday benediction on the crowd. They ate their fried apple pies during the Bethlehem pig race and exited through the gift shop, past hillbilly weather forecasters and rubber-band six shooters. The whole thing had been a letdown, and the grumbling in the minivan on the drive home made Melanie feel guiltier than ever.

Inevitably, Christmas Eve was here. Neither rain nor nerves nor squabbles had been able to stop it. The men were keen for the Christ Child's arrival in their own way and got off to an early start, taking a more celebratory, liquid, and less industrious path than their wives. Mom and Dad took all three teenagers and little Jennifer to see Santa—or all the kids took Mom and Dad, depending on one's point of view. The teenagers knew that Santa lived at a mall, so that was their attraction. Earl and Jim and Tom were anchored in front of the TV, taking turns through a succession of commercial breaks to get up, get beer, and then recycle it. Owing to basic chemistry, as the time drew nearer for them to actually go and pay their respects to the Lord in person, they were less and less ambulatory.

"These guys aren't going to want to go to church," Denise said, with a mixture of frustration and experience.

It was important to Melanie to pretend that this was not the case. She didn't want to mess up tonight too. Her teenagers had snuck out of going to church, and this was her last chance at the semblance of a real Christmas Eve. Her husband would have to come.

"Earl, we've got to be leaving in five minutes."

This had a tone of ultimatum. Earl hesitated and then said, "I'm…I'm not feeling so good, Mel."

Melanie pressed him. "What's the matter, honey?"

"My stomach." He could see that wasn't going to be enough, and added, "And my head. I've got a headache."

"Maybe a drive and some fresh air would do you some good," said Melanie, all the while staring at Earl's beer bottle.

He paused.

"I'm not going, Mel," said Earl.

Melanie turned away from him. She didn't want him to see the tears pooling in her eyes.

Defeated, she pulled the door slowly shut and walked down the stairs to join the other wives in the waiting minivan.

Tired but determined, Denise, Carol, and Melanie headed out to where the lady at the Piggly Wiggly told Melanie they'd find a Catholic church. You pass by all types of things at the beach, but you rarely pass by churches. They have them, all right; beach people are as God-fearing as any other. It's just that their churches don't usually take up prime real estate. So it was a long and unfamiliar drive that the women took as they sought to fulfill their traditional obligations. Eventually, at the end of the rough little two-lane road, three blocks behind an Old Time Pottery store, they came to a little church, its small parking lot already almost full. The sun was just going down.

"Hey, wait a minute," said Denise.

Looking out the windshield of the minivan, they read the name of the church together: "Shepherd of the Sea Assembly of God Church."

Carol looked at Melanie. "You did ask for a *Catholic* church, didn't you, Mel?"

There was an awkward silence.

"We can't go in there," Denise said.

"Why not?" asked Carol.

"You know," Denise said, her voice getting much, much younger. "We're not allowed to."

This was the last straw. Melanie couldn't even get Christmas Eve right. She burst into tears.

Denise and Carol both put their arms around her. They shushed her softly but let her cry.

Carol spoke again, this time more insistently. "Listen, it's a church, not a cathouse. And I want to go to church!"

Melanie wiped her eyes. She looked back and forth between the two women and then nodded. "Okay. Let's go." She left the van first, and the other two followed behind her.

They crossed the white gravel parking lot and entered in through the wooden double doors of the church. The place was just about packed, but there was a space for the three of them in a pew near the back of the sanctuary.

Having never set foot in "another" church, they had no way of knowing that this was more of a pageant than a normal service. They looked all about them at first, instead of looking toward the front. They were going through a little mental checklist: no holy water, no stained glass, no Stations of the

Cross. It's funny how the absence of things can make a place seem so strange.

"Look," Carol said, nudging her companions and directing their attention frontward with a tilt of her head.

The altar was decorated to look like a stable. Now besides the lack of the familiar, they had to deal with hay bales and a church that seemed more like a barn. The congregants finished up a hymn, and then turned to watch an open door to the left side of the altar. At a cue from the organ, a young man came through it, leading a girl seated on a donkey. The sisters-in-laws' eyes simultaneously grew wide. The boy was tall and thin and wearing a false beard. The girl looked even younger. The boy led the animal and the girl, who appeared to be quite pregnant, up a ramp and on to the main stage. Off the platform and out of sight, a woman was reading from Luke—*Saint* Luke, as the three visitors knew him—into a microphone.

"They're so *young*," Denise let out in a whisper. "They're just kids."

A shepherd appeared on the side of the stage, and together with the young man, helped the girl off the donkey. This same shepherd led the animal back through a curtain, while the couple disappeared behind the curtain on the opposite side. There was a pillow-ectomy offstage, and then the couple reappeared. The girl now held a quite small and very real baby wriggling in her arms. It only took one look from the girl to the baby, which she nestled tenderly into a V-shaped box lined with hay, for the women to realize that the child was actually hers.

"This is beautiful," Carol said. Melanie looked at her and then back at the stage. She was completely entranced.

This scene had taken place very slowly, with the music in the background softly underscoring the voice on the microphone. That voice stopped with the arrival of three men in robes carrying boxes. The trio bowed down in unison to the little baby snuggled in the manger. The music got just a tad louder as everyone on the stage froze and then ceased altogether. As this silent moment hovered above the congregation, all across the church people began to get up and applaud. The three visitors from Minnesota were soon standing and applauding with them. From the right side of the stage, a man in a blue suit and a red tie pushed out a lectern that had been hidden behind a stack of hay bales.

"This is Christmas, folks," he said gently, as everyone sat back down. "Real Christmas. A poor boy and a poor girl traveling to a distant, crowded city. Were they alone? Well, yes and no. The 'no' part is that the hand of God was always upon them, so they were never really alone. But that doesn't mean they couldn't feel lonely. Or even scared. And certainly they were tired and worn out." The pastor scanned the attentive congregation. "Why did those three wise men come? You know, they might have been wise, but they weren't perfect. The only perfect person there was that baby.

"The wise men weren't perfect, but they felt deep inside that they just *had* to come; they had to give what gifts they had, and give glory to God, and see their new king. But they were also *sent*. And when they did show up, they were also sent to help Mary and Joseph, two other imperfect people, as well. Christmas isn't just about what happened a long time ago. Christmas is alive and with us here today. Maybe our part of Christmas is to be imperfect people helping other imperfect people in honor of the Perfect One."

He paused a moment. Melanie leaned forward.

"Now I want us to do something special this Christmas," he continued. "Something to make this a *real* Christmas. We have the most loving congregation I know of. I'm always bragging to God about you people. But some of us are in need at this time of plenty, and I want the rest of us to show them that God still cares about them. Let us imperfect people love one another." He took a deep breath. "If you're here today and you have a need, a financial need, I want you to just raise your hand. And then close your eyes; close your eyes in faith. And folks, when you see a hand raised near you, I want you to walk over and put some money in it, you understand?"

There was a little rustling in the crowd, and it took a while, but then one hand went up on the far side of the church. A little while longer, and another hand went up. And then a third. Other people in the congregation began drawing to these upraised hands and pressing money into open palms. There were a lot of voices all at once, and Melanie was surprised, realizing that these people were praying out loud. The pastor at the lectern was praying, too, his eyes closed, his head bowed, both hands raised over his head.

And then, directly in front of Melanie, a girl with a partially shaved head and a black leather jacket meekly raised her hand. She had a trio of silver crosses in her right ear.

Melanie didn't hesitate. She plunged her hand into her purse and came out with a wad of bills. She reached forward and squeezed them into the young woman's hand.

Carol saw an elderly man with his upraised hand off to the other side of them. She and Denise made their way over to him and pressed money into his hand.

All of the women from Minnesota were crying.

After a while the lights came up, and the service—such as it was—melted into chatter and laughter. Everyone was talking to everyone else, and there was lots of hugging. Melanie and Carol and Denise took their place in a line of middle-aged women; eventually they all got a chance to hold baby Jesus.

Reluctantly, people began to filter out into the evening. Melanie had spied a little craft table as they came in. Among the reindeer potholders and the Santa trivets, there was a beautifully carved, wooden tree ornament: a nativity. She found the pastor and begged him to sell it to her. *Something new*, she thought to herself. He smiled and took her check. Melanie fingered over the details of the ornament—Mary, Joseph, the Child…and the three Wise Men. She gazed at it the whole quiet drive home.

Denise pulled the minivan back in between the big wooden pillars that supported the beach house. They were surprised to see that Mom and Dad were still out with all the kids—could they be having fun? The van's headlights glared into the empty carport. The women sat in the vehicle a few minutes, each in her own little Christmas, and then Melanie opened the door, triggering the dome light. The three of them walked up the stairs, lit by a single bright bulb at the top, and went inside.

The TV was as loud as ever, muffling the sound of the women's entrance. There was Earl in the kitchen, silhouetted in the ethereal light of the refrigerator, a new beer in his right hand. It seemed that he'd made a predictable recovery. Melanie walked up, unnoticed, behind her husband and touched his shoulder, startling him. Earl spun around, sending a little splash of beer sailing out of the top of the open bottle.

Melanie said ever so sweetly—and ever so genuine-ly—"Feeling better, honey?"

Earl fumbled to get up to speed and then said, "Oh, yeah. Yeah. I'm feeling much better, Mel."

"Me too," said Melanie. She stroked his cheek with the back of her hand. In her other hand was the nativity orna-ment. She held it up for him to see. "Isn't it beautiful?"

About the Author

Author photo by Chase Benton Photography

PIERCE KOSLOSKY, JR. GRADUATED WITH A degree in Psychology from Duke University. After working three years in North Carolina's maximum-security prison, he moved to Nebraska. Four decades later, he is the chairman and CEO of a manufacturing company. He lives in Omaha with Candy, his wife of thirty-five years, and with one very fortunate golden-doodle. They have four children who could not be more different!

Pierce and his family have gone to Surfside Beach, South Carolina for over twenty-five years. For most of that time they have stayed in the blue house on the cover of *A Week at Surfside Beach*. They bought the home in 2000 and rent it out in summer. Originally a poet, Pierce began writing these short stories fifteen years ago, inspired by entries in their guest book.